HOWL OF THE HUNTED

A NEW ORLEANS WEREWOLF NOVELLA

J.T. PATTEN

To Murphy, my dog.

Thank you for showing me the true ways of the alpha.
Sorry I neutered you, afterward.

A WARNING TO THE READER

This horror novella concerning the Rougarou (Werewolf) contains subject material that includes violence, abusive, and/or graphic scenes and descriptions some readers may find disturbing or triggering.

"Earth provides enough to satisfy every man's needs, but not every man's greed."

– Mahatma Gandhi

"We have doomed the wolf not for what it is, but for what we deliberately and mistakenly perceive it to be—the mythologized epitome of a savage, ruthless killer—which is, in reality, no more than a reflected image of ourself."

– Farley Mowat

PROLOGUE

Atchafalaya Basin Wetlands, Louisiana 18th Century

The moon, full and bright, exposed predators and prey within the murky bayou of the river delta. A sole silver eye hung in the sky, draping in its light the twisted roots of ancient cypress trees, like the spectral tendrils of Spanish moss that hung from the gnarled upper branches.

A hunter and his Acadian guide glided underneath the wetland canopy with each quiet oar stroke in their nocturnal journey through the swamp.

Still waters licked at the bow of the flat-bottomed wooden pirogue as it cut through the gentile current. Trailing ripples caused small flickers to meet the glowing gator eyes floating in wait for opportunities to feed by the shoreline.

Fireflies flitting above further illumed the passage through the narrow channel maze, drawing the stranger closer to the embrace of nature.

The night air was thick with hugging humidity, and the suffocating dampness behind the blanket of mosquitos enveloped all creatures great and small within the tangled labyrinthine of fresh and rotting vegetation. The potent scent of damp earth and gasses of decomposition mingled with the fragrance of blooming magnolias as the spirits breathed, infused the passing breeze with a marriage of an earthy sweet stench, relaying the ever-present cycle of life and death.

As the two men pushed the boat through the relative calm, the gentle lap of the water against the vessel joined in rhythm with croaking frogs, the occasional buzzing of nocturnal insects, and the rare howl of the red wolf in a somber chorus with eerie echoes that seemed to warn of unseen dangers.

The hoots of distant owls and mournful cries of soaring crows and hawks added a carnivorous layer to the already foreboding atmosphere and aural discord of sounds.

Feeling like the spot was right, the paid scout back-paddled the boat to turn into the weeds toward a small ridge line. The two men stepped off into the murky marsh, with watchful eyes on the Jurassic beasts drawing nearer, as their own footsteps sunk into the dangerous mire.

"Judas's silver," the local guide whispered aloud, French-Canadian accent thick. "I sell my soul but certain for your coin."

"Shhh," hushed the hunter, eagerly sloshing through the muck as if he was the one who knew the way. "You took the silver. Show me my prize."

A dense mist anchored to the ground once they waded past the waters, concealing treacherous potholes and sinkholes that threatened to swallow unwary souls. Wraith-like wisps of settled fog snaked their way around the men's legs as if the swamp itself sought to ensnare them in its clutches, to stop them from themselves.

Unwavering, the men pressed on, senses honed.

The guide was the first to catch a fleeting glimpse of movement amidst the tangled underbrush.

He raised his arm to halt.

There, bathed in the moon's soft radiance, stood the elusive wolf at the base of a tall rise. Its sleek silhouette melded with the shadows; yellow eyes gleaming with primal intelligence.

The beast paused, tilted its head back, and released a mournful howl that sent a shiver down the men's spines.

To the alpha's left, another wolf appeared from the lush growth, a tad slighter. Then trailed the small ones. Four cubs in total.

The guide pointed to the male and gave a knowing nod.

In that instant, time seemed to slow. His heart pounding, the hunter raised his rifle and brought his conquest into the long barrel's sight.

The moon, a backdrop to the impending drama, bore anxious witness to their encounter with a dimming shade of sad luminescence. Another wave of thin passing cloud cover offered to shroud the shame it could not bear to watch.

The encounter crackled with trepidation and exhilaration as the hunter and his quarry locked eyes.

In that haunted tableau, the hunter's finger curled around the warm trigger; walnut stock pulled tight to the shoulder, his breath held in tense anticipation.

He sucked in the sticky night air through a small crack in his lips.

The guide wheeled his head around, nervous. He wiped clammy hands on soaked pants.

The swamp, knowing their kind and the impending act of violence, rose to a crescendo of creature calls, desperately trying to dissuade him.

In the seconds that followed, the hunter's decision hung in the balance, his own existence entwined with the life of the majestic creatures before him.

His decision had been made hours before he set off in search.

He exhaled.

And then, in a split second...pulled the trigger.

A deafening crack shattered the ardent cacophony in the night, reverberating through the dense foliage.

The wolf popped at the sound nearly as quickly as the force doubled him over—dead in the brush.

With an instinct honed by centuries of evolution, his mate and her babies vanished into the inky blackness, eluding the hunter's deadly aim.

As the echoes of the gunshot faded away, the hunter waited as if alone in the moonlit swamp, his eyes fixed on the spot where the female and her litter had vanished.

"*Allons-y*. We must leave," coaxed the guide, his rush a clear sign of growing fear. "I'll get him for you. He'll make a fine skin."

The hunter grabbed his tracker by the shoulder and squeezed. "I want all of them."

"No. We mustn't. You've taken the male. No more."

The night sounds of frogs, owls, and other creatures gradually resumed their refrain, scolding the hunters, enraged by the killing.

Neither of the two expected the bitch to return as quickly, but there she was with the family in tow.

She approached her lying mate, cautious, crouched, afraid.

First, a sniff.

Then a lick.

A paw. A desperate claw.

She reared her head, scanning the swamp.

She howled, grieving her loss. The litter mimicked the grief.

"Please," the guide begged.

The hunter lifted his gun without a word. Another shot cracked the bayou. And then more. So many more, as fast as the hunter could fill and tamp, point and shoot.

The pups scurried around in panic but failed to seek refuge. One by one, they fell.

The calm of the night air grew to a torrent gale.

The hunter, unlike the French trappers who'd migrated from Canada, had no intentions of harvesting his kills for meat, hide, or bone. His quest was one of adrenaline and domination.

His guide, made uneasy by the deed and with the shift in

surroundings, fled, followed only by the slapping sounds of his feet to the ground.

The chirps, trills, and lisps of the disparate bugs and beasts converged into one. The sound was piercing. The night calls transformed into a pitch and pattern of mockery. Taunting the hunter, who twisted, reloaded, took aim, and fired at his deserting accomplice.

"Traitor," he said upon taking aim and drawing in the trigger slack.

Within the gunshot crack and an ensuing splash of the guide's death-fall, the volume of the bayou grew louder and repeated a pattern. A pattern that twisted and warped into an imitation of voices.

The hunter hastened his own retreat, pace quickening as the ghostly groans grew. He steadied a bouncing engraved hatchet at his side and cushioned occasional stumbles with his rifle tangling in tall grasses, slowing only to leap over his lifeless guide.

The swamp calls resonated faster. Clearer.

Take. And you must give.

Over and over the spectral voice of the swamp groaned.

Take. And you must give.

From his left.

The right.

Front.

Back.

The Crossroads kingdom opened. Spirits of nature, indigenous souls, and swamp witches all thrashed the hunter's senses as he rushed to the boat. Black animals gave chase as the hunter bolted.

Take. And you must give.

The moonlight burned through the ghostly obscurity, guiding his way, illuminating the path ahead as if by a turn of events, nature now conspired to aid in the escape.

But why?

∾

THE HUNTER AWOKE with a start at dawn.

He heaved a deep breath of relief.

How he'd returned unscathed was as thick in his mind as the fog he closely recalled navigating back to his home and family.

Turning to his wife's bed, his heart jumped, and the breath he'd expelled did not readily return.

He flipped from his mattress to his feet and rushed to her.

"Marie? Marie, wake up."

A bloodied heap lay on the floor. The torn gown was one he immediately recognized as one he'd given as an anniversary gift to his wife. Now it was shredded and sopping. He pulled at the soaked fabric to find his beloved. Rib cage split. Her hanging jaw was fractured, unhinged, and ripped to the side. Her abdomen ravaged and void. Legs broken akimbo, splintered and blue through her once milky skin.

As he howled in disbelief and sobbed when he could catch a breath, a new revelation struck him, and he collapsed at the nightmare's revelation—the children.

He sprung from the floor, roaring in panic as he raced to his children's room. "Christian? Thomas? Margaret?"

"Margaret!"

"OH GOD!"

"OH GOD!"

"No. No. No. No. This can't be."

They, too, were cast about in a similar broke and bloody butchering.

"Who would? How?" His hatchet, clean, was embedded deep into the wall. He paced in a circle around the heap of decimated, drained bodies.

"What the... my... oh, God. Who would do—?"

The hunter buried his head in his hands. Shaking, he clawed his fingers through his own hair, still unable to catch that desperate full breath.

It was then that he felt the wet stickiness on his hands, strands of hair curled around his fingers and stuck to his palm and in his crusted broken and torn nails. His hands moved against his will to his own mouth. He suckled his fingers and savored metallic aftermath in his mouth, coating his tongue and teeth with the liquid life of his family.

"No, this can't be."

Visions filled his reeling mind. He saw it. Saw it all clearly.

"Why would I—"

He struggled in vain to calm himself. Raising his head to catch the elusive air stuck behind his knotted heart. As his wind returned and filled his lungs, a smell rose to his nostrils. The familiar smell of the swamp and of a wet animal.

"The wolf," he breathed with heavy regret. The heaviness turned to a rapid pant. "This... for an animal?"

A buzzing emerged near his ear. Nay, a whisper. *There is more to give.*

~

IT WAS after one hundred and one days that the cursed hunter returned to a small desolate cabin in the bayou from his nightly cursed call in the marshes. Bloodied, coarse hair patches fell from his shifting skin. His sentence served, the hex would pass to another. At least that was what the voice of the Conjure Man coached through a black spectral shape like a guiding shadow in the night.

An unconscious poacher lay miles away, a large bite wound clotting and healing from the man's ravaged shoulder.

The hunter walked to the earthen circle he'd dug out earlier and emplaced a blackened lit candle. Melted into a ball within his other hand was what had once been a precious silver necklace he'd given his young daughter. It was one of the few objects he carried as he fled from killing his family months ago.

"Adja gebe o. Kutu adja gebe o," he recited eleven times, as instructed." He blew out the candle and turned it over, sinking it into the soft earth.

The hunter dropped the ball into a gunpowder-filled barrel, pressed the pistol to his temple, and fired.

As he fell, the wetlands spoke as they had before, the sounds of the swamp coming together in one voice.

You have given back to Damballah and Bondye, and commanded the same of another. He will protect Brother Bayou. This is the rebirth you have been fed.

1

Present Day Louisiana (August)

I t was as if the sun had taken a seat on a park bench to enjoy the day and relax, as the city buzzed with life. The bright ball of fire loitered in the sky, refusing to surrender its brightness to wherever it disappeared once its light left New Orleans. There was so much to do during the day that the sun couldn't do at night, not that it approved of the moon and the debauchery that happened under its watch.

L.J. Talbot had been watching that very sun set for what seemed like hours, alone in his thoughts. As he, his wife and daughter drove past the 'Welcome to Louisiana' sign from the Interstate, short and long shadows cast on fields, foliage, and riverbanks mesmerized him.

He was excited about the move. About the opportunity to hunt and fish. The chance to rub elbows with the bosses. A chance to look at short skirts for over three months of the year. To heed an internal calling to this very location that had been ricocheting inside of him for what seemed like a lifetime, though he couldn't fathom why aside from the raw nature and opportunities for trophies that existed along the waters.

He turned to his wife, Gwen, as she clipped her toenails in their spacious Range Rover while she hummed along to yet another goddamned Taylor Swift song on her AUX playlist, which comprised only twenty goddamn songs that had played on shuffle for the last four hours, and the last two years of their life when they were in the goddamn SUV she'd convinced him to buy. As if he had a choice.

He brought his eyes back to the road and the thought of escaping to the Louisiana marshland. He could leave it all behind. He tested himself in his mind if he could actually leave the only two living women in his life. Maybe it would be hard at first. Probably harder after a bit. Nah. He'd miss 'em, he resolved. L.J. hummed against the speakers, the Eagle's song, Hotel California.

For the first hours after leaving Chicago, L.J. and Gwen talked about his new job at the oil company. Gwen spoke enthusiastically about the rich and influential people they would soon rub shoulders with, her voice filled with anticipation. L.J. wondered to himself how big of an alligator he could snare—he contemplated getting a bear license—but most of all, he wanted to bag the black timber wolf the guys working the swamp gasses told him about. It was a true unicorn in a state that rarely had any wolves roaming, or indeed had none since the smaller red wolves started cross-breeding with coyotes.

Gwen popped her head up from her make-do pedicure. "Hey, Lair, let's drive down Bourbon and show Jenny the sights before we get to the house. I just texted the movers, and they still don't have beds set up yet."

Larry, or L.J. as everyone else called him, couldn't keep himself from counting his wife's toe nails dropping into the high pile car mats. "Sure," he replied flatly, both answering and turning the SUV off the interstate as she clipped and dropped and picked and rubbed and lotioned... and put her moist feet on the leather console while patting her thighs to the beat of Swift's Cruel Summer.

No shit, Taylor. Cruel indeed. His face wrinkled as his eyes fixed on her grooming remnants and the greasy smear on the leather. His mouth remained closed. *Just a little longer. Surrender me now.*

"Is there a parade today?" Jenny, his nine-year-old daughter, asked from the backseat, her nose pressed to the window, eyes fixed on the passing colors and architecture of the French Quarter neighborhood, herds of pedestrians walking about with hats and drinks and beads. She steamed the glass with her mouth, drew a smiley face, erased it, spelled her name, and repeated. Her eight-year-old stuffed bunny, Carrot, also had his stitched nose pressed to the window, clutched in the comforts of his little momma's little arms.

Gwen snapped her arm to her husband's and squeezed. They both looked at each other in jaw-dropping horror that rose to a grin and a giggle.

"Do you think?" Gwen asked. Her face contorted.

L.J. shook his head. "It's not Mardi Gras or Jazz Fest, but..." He shrugged, puffed a breath, and laughed. "The beads flow freely. Not like she's a boy. Doubt her head will spin around if she sees a couple of boobs."

"Like you." Gwen slapped him on the arm playfully, then went back to clipping. "That doesn't happen in the day here, though, does it?"

He smiled. "Hope so." And winked. He stretched his arm to her shirt buttons, extending a finger through the cloth to her bra covered bosom.

"Pig. That's why you took a detour to cut through the Quarter. I know you." She slapped his hand away, turned the radio up. One of her favorite songs was replaying. Again. With a snip, a flying nail crossed the console, landing in her husband's lap.

"JEEZUS!" L.J. dropped his hands from the wheel, brushing his lap frantically like he'd seen a spider crawling up his thighs.

"Oh, my God. Overreact much?" Her brow was bent, eyes hard, as she picked the nail up from his leg, then flicked it to his feet. Her gaze leveled and widened in fresh horror. "Larry!"

Jenny screamed. "Daddy!"

The SUV came to a screeching halt, but not before hitting something large and dark. The figure bounced from the grill to the pavement and rolled to the French Quarter gutter gravy, where it lay still in the filth of beer, vomit, green grenade juice, and who knows what else.

L.J. popped from the car, cursing.

"Is he dead? Daddy, is he dead?" Jenny called out, wiping a small trailing tear from her cheek with Carrot's floppy ear.

"Stay here," Gwen ordered her daughter while exiting from her side and rounding the car. "You weren't even paying attention, Larry. What the hell did you do?"

"ME? Don't Larry, me. You're the one distracting me by spreading your disgusting toe jam all over the car. Flicking your toe cheese nail clippings all over everyone." L.J. bent to examine the man, careful not to soil his own khakis as he checked for signs of life. "I barely hit him." L.J. looked around. He lowered his voice. "Shit, we're being watched. Don't turn around."

Gwen turned her head back and forth with concern.

"Never mind listening to me."

"Is he dead?" she asked. Then pivoted to the most pressing concern. "If the front end is damaged, we should call insurance right away. Do you remember how much the deductible is?"

"How should I know? I just don't want the cops to come."

"Oh, my god. You could get arrested. Like for manslaughter." Gwen pointed from a safe distance. "Check his pulse. If he's alive, he'd have to press charges."

The man laid out on the pavement was no doubt from the streets. His pores oozed the smell of booze and musky sweat like a wet dog. Skin burnt, tanned, and leathery. It was probably a hundred degrees, and he wore long pants and a hoodie. An unkempt beard almost hid his scratched and raw skin. L.J. was sure it wasn't road rash. Maybe scabies. Could be meth jitters.

"Lair, did you check his pulse? You better not end up in jail for being a shitty driver. Do his neck. We're going to have to pay extra if the movers are just waiting."

"Do I look like a fucking doctor? Put my hand near his face and he could bite me."

"No, you don't look like a doctor, you look like an asshole, but I'm not asking you to shit on him. Grab his arm or his neck. You check your own pulse every time you walk up the stairs, and it's not near your big fucking mouth."

Shadows emerged from dark enclaves, some hustling over like a crab walk. Others, like crooked toys, wobbled a few feet further before their batteries gave out.

"He okay, he okay," one of the approaching figures said. Raspy, weak, but assured. "C'mon, Jean. Up you go. Dat okay. Dat okay." The man leaned into his friend and sniffed. "Yeah, he okay."

The others crowded L.J. and Gwen, the stench overpowering. Their dirty, scabbed hands clawed at and shook their friend. "Let's go, Jean. C'mon, boy. We get you right."

The man's eyelids lifted as they roused him to consciousness. The whites around his dilated pupils and auburn irises were bloodshot and jaundiced yellow. He smiled a toothless grin. "I taut I got hit by a moose, I did."

The men on the street all laughed.

"Dat moose come runnin' out at me. He says, 'move out da way, I coming through.' Like he fleein' da swamps, Mister Rougarou hot on his tail."

His friends roared in delight. "Least we know he ain't looking fo us, dats what I know."

One added as he laughed, "Back in Chauvin and Lake Barre, I ain't neva ate no moose when I was da wolf. You?"

The smiles froze. All eyes dropped.

Gwen and L.J. turned about with a '*Who farted?*' look.

Silence.

Another of the street buddies spoke up after the long pause. "You folks be on your way. He okay. Just a scratch. He okay. Maybe you give him a little something case he hasta see a doctor or something. Fancy car like that. Probably has a couple dollars for big gas tank. Ya hear me, my baby?"

Gwen touched L.J., giving him an approving nod. "That's a good idea, Lair. You have some cash?"

L.J. nodded. "Maybe five, ten bucks? Guessing you guys don't take Venmo or Chase Pay?" He reached into his pant pocket, pulling a couple of wadded receipts, a five, and two singles.

His wife shook her head. "I may have a few dollars in my purse. Hang on." She quick-stepped, still barefoot, back to the car.

"Mommy, did Daddy kill that man?"

"No, Jenny. He's fine. He's just homeless. I'll be right back," she said, flipping through a small stack of twenties in her wallet, deciding to take three of them, putting one back. She reached for her shoes, lifted her feet to inspect the bottoms, and decided otherwise. The pavement was cooling as the sun slipped away. "Here," Gwen said, folding the twenties in half and adjusting the corners to look like more. "And add to this what you have. We still need to tip the movers."

L.J. nodded. He handed the small wad to the man recovering on the curb and now sitting upright. The group was still quiet.

"You sure you're okay?" L.J. asked. "We can call an ambulance if you need—"

"Lair, we need to go. I'm afraid Jenny may need to go to the bathroom soon. I have to pee, too."

"Mama, I don't have to–"

"Shhh. Roll up that window. You just told me you had to go."

The man waved with the back of his hand. "You go on, now. I okay. If I need you, I'll track you down." He looked up at Gwen and then at Jenny, her face in the window. Then he turned to L.J.

"Dats a real pretty little girl you got dere." The man nodded and lowered his eyes to the street. "Real beautiful family, yes, sir. You hold 'em tight. One ting about a man, they fight like the devil when day family gets took. A lady, she do her fightin' every day to keep tings in order. Dats why she do what she do. Dat's why you need to give her more loving so you can mate for life."

"Ew. Okay, gross. Let's go." Gwen turned, pointed at her daughter, then spun her fingers, mouthing, *turn around*, before getting back in the car.

L.J. patted the man on the shoulder. "Good talk," he said, and walked away. "Guess that's why all you guys are still married with those pro-tips." Larry feigned looking around, "Yeah, no wives."

The man grinned at L.J. while waving a bent, bony finger. "You gon live a long time here. I hears the voices. Someone talkin' 'bout you. Could be da Lutain. The trickster, my baby. Could be da spirits and the Conjure Man. Dey gone do you proper, sha. You should never come down to dis boot. Papa Leghba he lookin' fo you. He be wearing his gator head, if you lookin' out."

~

FOR THE NEXT FEW MINUTES, short of Gwen wiping at her feet with a wad of napkins from the glove box, and complaining of how gross the street was, the car was silent. Somewhere between the near roadkill of the homeless man and them setting off again, even Taylor Swift had stopped her complaining and rage.

"Why is it so hot?" Gwen moaned, fanning herself. "Oh, God, Jenny, roll up your window. Why is it down? It's too hot."

"I gave the man Carrot."

"YOU WHAT?" They shouted from the front seats in unison as L.J. slammed the brakes.

Not answering, Jenny replied, "Where do these people all live?" Her voice was filled with innocence and compassion as she pointed to a group of homeless individuals huddled together under a bridge.

"Should I go back?" L.J. asked.

Gwen's face scrunched. "And give that filthy thing back to your daughter? Nice."

"Jenny," L.J. said. "We'll get you a new one. Did we get that on Amazon or an actual store?"

"I don't know. But that's your answer? Buy more? She needs to learn a lesson." Gwen turned. "You need to be more careful with your possessions. You don't just give away your things. They're expensive."

Jenny pointed. "Those people, too. Under the road, sitting in the bridge shadows. Are they homeless like the man daddy almost killed?"

"I didn't almost kill him. He's fine."

Gwen glanced in the direction Jenny was pointing and sighed softly. "Oh, sweetheart, those men we were helping, they're just less fortunate than we are. They don't have a home like we do," she explained, her voice laced with sympathy.

"We're privileged," L.J. added with a smirk. "Get comfortable with that word."

Jenny frowned, her young brows furrowing in contemplation. "But why don't we help them, Mommy? Shouldn't people all stick together, like animals do? Animals take care of each other like Native American indigenous tribes used to."

L.J. chuckled from behind the wheel, his eyes focused on the road ahead. "Native American and indigenous in the same breath. Looks like we got our taxes worth this year in your education. It's not that simple, kiddo," he added, his voice carrying a note of skepticism. "You see, in most animal groups, there's an alpha, a leader who calls the shots. But when that alpha gets old or weak, others challenge and kill him to take his place. Old females often get left behind. Places like where we're moving to, in the swamps, alligators, bears, and boars eat them. Circle of life. These people in the streets are just weaker. They aren't alphas, their like...zetas or something."

"That's a Mexican gang," Gwen corrected.

"That's not fair," Jenny whispered, her voice barely audible. "No one's going to eat them. And Mommy showed me the pictures of the house. It's not in the swamp. It's in a neighborhood. Maybe they could make a tent in our backyard so the cars going by don't wake them up."

L.J. glanced at Jenny through the rearview mirror, his expression pensive. "That's just how it goes, dumpling."

"Chinese people treat their old with respect," Jenny said with a renewed voice.

He retorted, "They also eat homeless dogs and kill second-born daughters. Don't cherry-pick your facts."

The young girl crossed her arms. "You're lying."

"Am I lying?" He turned to Gwen for support.

Eyes on her mobile device, she nodded. "Daddy's not lying, dumpling. Mommy saw it on Tik-Tok. Dogs in cages and then boiled alive. Monsters. I watched one and had it on my feed for a week. So gross."

"Thank you." L.J. looked back to the mirror. "It might seem like a blessing to be homeless and have the freedom to do as you please, but if you can't step up, you may not get the support and protection of a community, and life can be much harder. It's best if you contribute to the whole before taking from others. That's just a good law of life."

Jenny squinted her eyes, processing the reply. "Are you a Republican or a Democrat?" When no answer came, she returned her gaze to the window. "Bye, Carrot. Hope you like your new *not* home."

The car rounded a corner, and the luxury of the Garden District loomed before them. Even in the diminishing light, the grand houses and immaculately fenced yards were a stark contrast to the scenes they had just witnessed.

Gwen twisted herself to her daughter in the back seat. "Don't worry, sweetie," she said, her voice filled with warmth and reassurance. "We're fortunate to have each other and a safe place to call home. It's important to remember to help those in need when we can, even if we can't solve all of their problems. But that's usually done through taxes. Mommy gave the man Daddy almost killed some money to help him if he needs medical attention or something else to make his pain and troubles go away. That was totally going above and beyond what we already do."

L.J. turned to his wife. "Stop."

"Hey," she threw her hands up in mock surrender, "if he wants to get more drugs and kill himself, that's on him. He'll probably be dead in a week if he doesn't die of internal injuries."

"He'll probably choke on one of your toenails."

From the rear, blocking out her parent's laughter, Jenny nodded slowly, her eyes fixed on the passing houses. The weight of the conversation lingered in the air, a subtle reminder of the disparities that exist in the world. As their car pulled into their new driveway, Jenny cast one last glance at her own reflection in the glass, then looked to the rearview mirror to look at her father's eyes.

He winked and mouthed *I love you* with an air kiss.

2

Garden District Next Morning

Sweat dripped from Gwen's bent brow. It seeped from her forehead, behind her ears, and beaded on her nose. "Fuck, Lair. Just fuck!"

A *functional* air conditioner differed from an effective one, which was one of the many unpleasant surprises of the move as L.J. and Gwen continued their tireless efforts to unpack boxes in their new home. Beads of sweat trickled down L.J.'s temple as he lifted yet another heavy carton, grunting under its weight. The move had taken its toll on them both, but they were determined to settle into their new life. Unexpected promotions only came around so often, so they thought it best to seize it when offered, and he'd caught Gwen in a good mood from the time he first proposed the idea all the way to the point when they'd crossed the state line. She'd not seen the heat and humidity in the pictures of the house options the realtor had shown them.

L.J. fanned himself with a fast-food menu by an open window

that offered no breeze. "I told you, none of the HVAC services I looked up are open. They'll call when they get my message."

Jenny sat cross-legged on the kitchen floor, munching on powdered sugar beignets. The white dust clung to her fingertips, leaving messy trails across the hardwood floors and into the deep plank crevices. Gwen watched her with exasperation, her eyes narrowing as she surveyed the growing mess.

"Jenny, sweetheart, can you please eat those over the table?" Gwen asked, her voice a mixture of irritation and weariness. She turned to her husband. "You didn't check to see if the owners might fix these canyons' cracks between the boards before buying, did you? You need to get that fixed."

L.J. rolled his eyes at the growing list of shithead decisions from the morning.

Jenny looked up, her big blue eyes shining with innocence. "But, Mom, the table is covered with boxes. I'll make an even bigger mess!"

Gwen sighed and rubbed her temples at the reminder. "Just try your best, Jenny, okay? Maybe eat on the porch?"

"It's too hot," Jenny replied. She wiped her forehead, smearing powdered sugar under her pulled-back hairline. "Can we get a swimming pool?"

L.J. wiped his brow with the back of his hand just as his daughter had done, catching his breath after moving a box from the kitchen to what would be the dining room. "Hey, honey," he said, voice slightly muffled, "I think I found a solution to our cleaning woes. I can go to the store and get a Swifter box of floor wipes. They'll make it easier to tidy up. Maybe they even have a small wading pool she can put her feet in. I can always pick up some Topo Chico for you. Seltzers could make the chores more of a party."

Gwen's eyes brightened, grateful for the suggestion. "That would be great, thank you. I have yet to see cleaning supplies in these boxes yet, and yeah, see if you can find the variety pack with the pineapple. Maybe that would lighten the mood. I know I've been kinda cranky this morning."

"I'll own that I haven't been too supportive and could've tempered my enthusiasm a bit to consider your feelings and needs." He put an insincere hand to his heart.

"Get the fucking drinks, Lair. Don't Dr. Phil me."

"Done!" L.J.'s enthusiasm waned slightly as he hesitated. "Actually, while I'm out, I was thinking I could swing by the hunting outfitters and see if they have any good deals on gear. I mean, once work starts, I won't have much time to do that kind of stuff, you know?"

"And there we have it. The real motive. God forbid you were just being nice." Gwen's smile faded, suspicion clouding her features. "Big surprise." She tossed her hands up. "All this to do, and you need to find a hunting guide, right? Can't think of anything or anyone else but yourself. Air conditioning repair isn't open in the Deep South, but by God, the bait shops and swamp safari people are."

"I got them donuts today, already, without you asking, and figured you'd like a cold drink." L.J. shifted uncomfortably, his gaze fixed on the floor. "I figured I could use the opportunity since I'll be out, anyway. Kill two birds with one stone. That's actually considering you, so I don't go out twice."

Gwen shook her head, a mixture of annoyance and resignation on her face. "Fine, but just an hour or two. Don't get carried away; we still have plenty to do here. I'm guessing they don't have phones or websites, so yeah, you'll probably need to drive quite a way to find one since that's the most important thing to do today. Clearly."

L.J. grinned sheepishly, relief washing over him. "Thanks, Gwen. I promise I'll be back before you know it."

"Whatever. Better answer your phone if the repair company calls."

As L.J. made his way to the front door, Jenny, clutching a slightly flattened beignet in her small hands, piped up inquisitively, "Daddy, why do you like hunting so much? Animals are happy with their families in the woods. Why do you want to hurt them and kill two birds?"

L.J. paused, smiling at her misconstrued meaning as his hand rested on the doorknob. He turned back to face her, his expression softening. "I don't hurt them, sweetheart. They don't feel a thing. Besides, sometimes animals have too many babies, and if there are too many of them, they can't all survive. So, hunters help keep their population under control. We could drive along, and an overpopulated area with deer could cause an accident. Could get us killed. You wouldn't want that, would you?"

Jenny's brows furrowed as she pondered L.J.'s words. "But if cities get too crowded, would animals ever hunt humans to keep their population down? A person jumped out from the road at our car. Should he be hunted?"

L.J. chuckled, his eyes filled with melancholic amusement. He crouched down to Jenny's level, placing a hand on her shoulder. "That was an accident. We've gone over this already. And no, sweetheart, animals don't hunt humans like that. We're different. We have our own ways of dealing with population control, but not boiling them. But hunting, for some people, is a way of connecting with nature. Getting back to our own primitive roots. Doing things with our senses and relaxing from day-to-day stress."

"By killing? Can't you just take a picture of the animals on a hike instead of killing them and taking pictures of them with silly hats and sunglasses?"

Gwen stopped unpacking and whipped her head around. "Honey, where did you hear about this?"

Jenny bit into her beignet and shrugged. When she'd swallowed, she said, "The boys at school showed me. Madison Murphy said my Daddy was a murderer. Her mom said it, too, when they drove us home from dance." Jenny shrugged again. "That's why I wanted to move. Here, no one knows Daddy, so they won't have seen his pictures making fun of dead animals."

Hands on his hips, L.J. huffed. "Madison Murphy's mom has killed half the blowfish in the Pacific with all her Botox."

Jenny rotated the beignet and bit a small corner with another shrug. "She doesn't put sunglasses and silly hats on them when they're dead."

L.J. swallowed hard, sans beignet. It was a tough pill of reality to take, especially from his own daughter. He nodded in understanding but turned away and walked out the door. No one knew that killing filled the emptiness he had inside from childhood. It gave him control where he felt he had none, in life. Even L.J. hadn't fully come to terms with it as a coping addiction.

"Don't forget to track down and bring back the seltzers, killer," Gwen called out with a gleeful chuckle.

L.J. said nothing back. His attention was focused on a curious pile of rice and pennies on the lower steps of the house.

THE DRIVE OUT of the city, as he headed southeast, was less head-clearing than L.J. had hoped. *Animals kill each other every day, and no one says a thing.* He does it, and his kid thinks he's a killer. People all over America kill deer and moose, get them mounted and put hats on them. He just did it in the wild. *People love it,* he assured himself. He had about twenty thousand followers after the caribou kill. *I mean, that was funny. Baseball hat between horns and cigar in the beast's mouth. Well, no one down south is going to raise a fuss. Hell, the kids are probably all wearing camouflage in school, not that they aren't a hundred miles out of Chicago, either.*

As he wrestled with both his rationale and his conscience, he monitored the map display that guided him to one of half a dozen gator tour and adventure guides he'd found online. With plenty of pictures of stacked dead alligators and piles of feral swamp boars in the boats posted on their sites, he knew no one would judge him for seeking a sporting guide for a hunt and a little photo shoot. *I'm going to give the people what they want. Something really wild.*

Within twenty minutes, he'd turned down a gravel road that wound him past modest and makeshift houses, some of which were little more than dilapidated trailer homes on river-front lots, with flaky paint shrimp boats, pickup trucks, airboats, and royal blue presidential Trump flags. When he saw the sign for Cajun Critter Adventures, he knew he was in the right place.

There were a few pickup trucks and a police car in front of the facility, and quite a few airboats docked on the water. In what looked like a series of live bait shops nailed together, L.J. opened a rickety wooden screen door with a swinging spring that no longer sprung. He pulled it closed with a loud creak as he walked in. A pungent odor somewhere between a fish shop and dog kennel stopped him midstride. Heads and eyes turned to him. He gave a polite nod as he held his breath, then awkwardly strolled around, looking at hunting photos and the stuffed wild game that adorned the walls, shelves, and displays. There were raccoons, alligators, foxes, boar, a small black bear, and plenty of deer. He sipped air through his mouth, trying not to breathe through his nose.

Yes, sir, he was in the right place, although as an outsider, he felt out of place amidst the local hunters and enthusiasts who seemed to know each other well, joking loudly with one another against what may have been a decade old display counter now securing a sole empty Doritos bag and worn edge stack of AAA maps. With a hint of uncertainty, he continued to wander through the tour shop, observing the assortments of hunting gear and wildlife-themed memorabilia on display, hoping someone would ask if he needed help instead of him having to interrupt.

Unbeknownst to L.J., three seasoned local guides and the county sheriff had been observing him from a distance. They exchanged amused glances, their eyes twinkling with mischief as they whispered jokes at his expense to one another. They could tell he was a fish out of water, his discomfort apparent as he hesitated near the bear hunting section where he toyed with a crossbow, giving it an approving nod, then fumbling with the crank cock device.

"You in the market for dat Barnett over dere? Break it, you buy it," said the shop owner, Beau Landry.

L.J. turned to the voice, not knowing which of them had spoken up.

Another local, Dale Doucet, waved him over, curiosity piqued by his presence and the courage he seemed to muster.

Despite his efforts, L.J. looked like a shy pup, avoiding direct eye contact.

With friendly smirks, they motioned for him to join their circle, where they leaned against the counter, sizing him up.

"Hey, thanks. I'm just nosing around. Had a couple questions, though. I like your shop," L.J. said, resting his hands on the counter and breaking a toothy smile to the small crowd. "Cool mounts."

"Shoot your wad, buddy. What brings you here?" the sheriff asked, a playful tone in his voice. "Take a picture with a swamp monster gator in da brown water. Get a little chicken ad sausage gumbo. Sha, c'est bon. Wanna coke? Which kind you want? We got Dr. Pepper, cokes here."

L.J. swallowed nervously, his gaze shifting from one person to another. Clearly, he was gathering his thoughts, trying to find the right words. After a moment of hesitation, he finally spoke up. "I—I was wondering if you offer bear or other exotic hunting opportunities around here?"

The locals exchanged cautious glances, the twinkle in their eyes replaced by a touch of suspicion. The sheriff raised an eyebrow, studying L.J. intently as he shifted his weight to rest a hand on the holster at his side.

"Bear hunting, huh? That's an unusual request," said Beau. "You see, the state no longer allows bear hunting, and I don't think the new law passed yet for a population control season. Ain't that right, Sheriff Gaudet?"

"That's right, Beau. Ten thousand dollar fine, as of now."

"How about a boar?" one man asked, elbow on the counter, hand to his chin. "We can do crossbow, pistol. You can slap a feral pig's ass in a clown suit. Whatever your fancy. As far as exotics, you can't shoot no Mexican or Bangkok strippers or nothin' neither."

The group laughed.

L.J. chuckled along.

"Where you stayin'? You ain't from here, boi," one of them asked.

L.J. felt a flush of embarrassment creeping up his neck. He knew his behavior had already given away that he wasn't native to the area. However, he tried to regain his composure. "Well, I just moved here recently," he replied, his voice laced with a hint of defensiveness. "So, I guess I'm a local now. Always felt drawn here. Kinda like it was home before it came to be. Know what I mean?"

"That wasn't a question. It was an observation. You won't ever be a local here. Not if you're here for ten years. Not if your name isn't on the plaque. I'm on the plaque. Robichaud. Sheriff Gaudet, he on the plaque. Landry. Even Dale's family, day on de plaque."

L.J. looked around the room, searching the walls. "What plaque?"

"Bien des Acadiens de l'Amerique du Nord descendent des familles dénombrées dans le recensement Acadie 1671," recited by rote, the local John Pitre as he picked at his teeth and spit whatever was between them on the floor.

Blank-faced, L.J. raised his shoulders. "I... uh, I don't know what that means."

"Der you go. You ain't on the plaque," said John. "You can't even read the plaque if it was starin' at your nose."

"Hah. Yeah," L.J. said. "Well, plaques or no plaques, I think we'll be here quite a while. No bear. That's a shame. I coulda sworn I read somewhere—"

"Read wrong. I can hardly read, and I read that. Wanna shoot a gator? That's exotic. Says so on the boots. Thirty-day license coming up starting this week. We got plenty of tags."

L.J. nodded. "I'd like that. Really, I would. So, thank you. Thank you for that option. But you see, big game hunting has always fascinated me, and I heard this region had some remarkable opportunities. Like, say, a wolf if bears aren't an option."

The locals couldn't help but exchange another round of skeptical glances. Dale Doucet put a large pinch of tobacco behind his lip and spoke up, a wry smile on his lips. "Son, you've got it all wrong. No wolves in Louisiana. Even if there were, hunting them would be illegal. We're actually trying to bring them back, you know?"

L.J.'s eyes widened in surprise. "But... but I heard rumors of a black timber wolf spotted in this area," he insisted, a flicker of determination in his gaze, his bravado returning.

The locals chuckled, their laughter tinged with a touch of disbelief. "You must've heard some tall tales, my friend," the sheriff remarked. "And even if there was one, don't mean it's yours to kill."

Beau raised his arms high and spread his fingers wide. "Better watch yer toes."

"Dat's what I was thinking, Beau. Better watch yer toes," parroted Dale.

The sheriff chuckled and continued, "You sure you're not reading up on Canada? This here is Louisiana, friend." He leaned further on the counter. "Trust us, stick to fishing and take up an alligator tour; that's where the genuine excitement lies in these parts. If that's why you moved here, I suggest you repack yer boxes and get them movers back in the house."

L.J. felt a pang of disappointment, realizing his request had met a dead end. However, he wasn't ready to give up just yet. "I can't. I moved here. Oil company. I understand if there really isn't a season or opportunity, but you see, I'm an experienced big game hunter," he said, his voice resolute. "If there's even a chance to hunt that black wolf, I'm willing to pay for the opportunity. No matter the cost."

"Well, you may be right there," the sheriff replied. "You'll pay, alright, more than the oil companies do for our land."

"Oh, trust me, I can pay," L.J. scoffed. He looked around the small shop. "I can pay for about anything in here and anything on whatever menu you have for hunting."

Dale shook his head. "I don't think you ready to pay so much."

L.J. stepped in closer to the men. "I'll pay anything."

"You come here with family?" Beau added. "Wife and kids?"

L.J. nodded yes. "Wife and daughter. My wife won't care what it costs. I spend my money on my things, and she spends my money on hers. God knows she has enough purses and Starbucks pink drinks."

The sheriff scratched his chin thoughtfully.

"Hell, right about now, I'd settle for shooting a crow," L.J. confessed.

The sheriff kicked at an old black piece of gum stuck on the floor. "You must not know much about wolves, after all. You always want to look for a murder of crows. Not the murder you're thinking. If wolves are back, they follow the crows. When the crow winks down at them, the wolf attacks. Both eat. You'll never see a wolf eat a crow. You'll never see a wolf hunter kill a crow."

L.J. raised his hands in mock surrender. "I'm just saying I want to hunt something. Bad. Like real bad. But something different from everyone else's posts."

"Posts?" Beau didn't look like he grasped the term but recognized the unwavering persistence. "Well, you're certainly all fixed with dat notion in your head. I'll give you that. But I can't promise anything. Wolves or not, hunting them in these parts isn't something we do. Man like you, though, almost sounds drawn here, like no reason gonna stop you. I'm gonna say this again. You might want to reconsider your options. Specially, since we about a hundred days."

"Oh, it's a hundred days, Beau. Hundred-one might make tonight."

The sheriff's face tightened. He didn't say a word. Instead, he looked out of the window as if looking for something, someone.

L.J. tried to follow the exchange. "A hundred days? Does the hunt start now? Is that what you're saying but not saying?" L.J. winked. "I can play along." He reached back for his wallet.

"Don Jay and his boy just down a ways went after the reds, but they were after their herd. Coulda been those coyote hybrids. Took three calves, so they thought, till they realized it was a gator. Caught em, too. Nose to tail, big monster dat one was."

L.J. nodded, a glimmer of determination still shining in his eyes. He understood that his request was an unusual one. "Look, if it's about them not being edible or anything, I don't want to eat em. I can't even eat meat." He lifted his shirt and patted his colostomy bag. "Bowel cancer, twenty-twenty. Rang the bell, knock on wood," which he did, on the glass counter. L.J. smiled. "I just like to shoot 'em and snap a photo for my socials. I have about five thousand followers at any point in time asking me to do something really crazy, and I'm not one to disappoint. Sometimes, I do something silly, like pretend to ride what I kill or put sunglasses or a hat on them. You know. Fun stuff. I was thinking I could use one of those Mardi Gras hats with the bells. I mean, that's some funny shit."

No one laughed.

L.J. checked his watch. He wasn't going home yet. His phone rang. A.C. could wait until the conversation was over, and sent it to voice-mail. He could feel that he was on to something. They seemed to like him, or so he convinced himself.

"What's your name, anyhow, Mr. Outsider?"

Hands on hips, L.J.'d had about enough of the name game. Time was ticking. "L.J. My name's L.J. Talbot. I'm from Chicago. Well, the North Shore. My grandfather told me stories of his brother who had family here years ago. Generations, I think. Went by our old name, Thibadeau. Not sure why they changed it. Anyway. That's who I am. Just good ole L.J. Talbot, hashtag LJTalbotHunts."

The locals looked at each other wide-eyed, with awakened faces of revelation and concern.

Beau muttered, "Shit. Dat boy, he on de plaque."

The sheriff blew out a deep breath. "Here we go again."

3

L.J. received no special treatment at the drop of old family ties. They all but kicked him out, perhaps faster than he thought they would've once everything was out in the open.

Back in the vehicle, his quest ending with no reward, L.J. convinced himself the first stop was probably just a bad stop of territorial locals who were happier just sitting around jawing than making an honest day's dollar—until he made four more stops that yielded the same results. Wild pigs, waterfowl, deer, armadillos, coyotes, squirrels, and rabbits, yes. Alligators in the next few days, yes. Bear and wolves, not a chance.

His phone rang again. He was already three hours late. Time to pay the piper. "Hi, hon. I'm coming home now. No hunting for me, so please, can we just leave it there without a fight?"

"You sound pretty down, babe," Gwen said. "I'm sorry it didn't work out."

"Thanks, I appreciate your understanding."

There was a relaxed pause. "Lair, the only thing I understand is that you're going to do what you want, when you want, wherever you want, no matter what I say. So, you know where I am?"

"I know. You're still stuck at home with all the boxes. I'm—"

"Nope." Gwen made a loud slurping sound. "Jenny and I checked into the Royal Sonesta Hotel in the French Quarter and are sitting poolside. Her with a Piña Colada smoothie and me with a Hurricane cocktail. And guess what, babe? I'm not coming home until you unpack all those fucking boxes, call the locksmith to change the locks, like I asked, and get the air conditioner fixed, as well as anything else you overlooked so you could move us to a new job, which it sounds like was more about hunting than your family. I'm not coming home until it's done. Bye!" She signed off with false cheeriness.

L.J. slapped the steering wheel. "Bitch!"

As he suffered a mini tantrum in the car, he missed his turn.

Google Maps attempted to redirect.

L.J. turned off on what looked like the correct route but was redirected again.

"What the fuck! I turned where you told me to." He turned again.

Recalculating route.

"You stupid fucking piece of shit!" L.J. floored the accelerator on a dirt road lined with dilapidated shacks and huts, trying to get back to the primary route but ultimately drawing himself deeper into the wilds.

For another fifteen minutes, the Range Rover trekked along the winding country roads of the Louisiana bayou, its tires kicking up dust in its wake. Derelict shacks, abandoned homes, and weathered trailers passed by, standing as testaments to forgotten dreams and discarded hopes.

The quiet drive was occasionally shattered by barking dogs, their eyes wild with territorial fervor as they chased after the passing car and the clouds it left behind. Their turf warnings echoed through the air, reminding L.J. that he was out of his element no matter how badly he sought to connect with it.

Above the vehicle, a congregation of birds soared across the boundless sky, their silhouettes casting fleeting shadows upon the sun-drenched earth. Majestic, winged predators soared with outstretched wings, their sharp eyes scanning the terrain below. Hawks, with their piercing gaze, circled high above, ever watchful. Vultures, ominous and patient, perched on the skeletal branches of the dead trees that lay scattered on the wasteland, their presence a macabre reminder of life's transience.

The sun beat down mercilessly upon the Rover, transforming its interior into a sweltering oven. The air conditioning struggled to keep up as it offered a brief respite from the oppressive heat. L.J.'s hands clung to the steering wheel, slick with perspiration, as his eyes squinted against the blinding sunlight his visor couldn't block.

With each passing mile, the bayou seemed to weave its spell, drawing L.J. deeper into its enigmatic embrace. The landscape, simultaneously haunting and captivating, held an ancient wisdom that whispered through the rustling leaves and trickling waters. It was a world that was, in some parts, untouched by time, a place where forgotten stories and legends murmured in the breeze. If he'd opened his window and succumbed to the heat, he might've heard their warnings.

Soon, L.J.'s frustrated thoughts turned introspective, contemplating the history buried within these swamplands. He wondered about the lives that once thrived in the forsaken homes surrounding him and the dreams that had taken root but withered away. There was a sense of melancholy, a bittersweet nostalgia that permeated the air, and a strange familiarity within the mystery. He wished he'd asked more about his distant family that once called this strange place home.

As the old SUV pressed onward, its engine humming with determination, L.J. felt a growing kinship with the bayou. It was a place of contradictions, where beauty and desolation danced together in a delicate balance. The bayou held secrets buried deep within its murky depths, waiting patiently to be discovered by those who dared to venture into its heart.

L.J. continued his endeavor until the road was no more.

Dead end.

He turned around and made a right where his intuition told him was the proper direction. The road was wet and peppered with large rain-filled potholes. The dirt soon became mud, and L.J. soon came to another dead end. He turned his wheel to make another turn. The SUV slid and stuck. He shifted the drivetrain, but the SUV sank deeper into the treacherous mud, its tires spinning futilely, churning up a whirlpool of frustration. He cursed under his breath, anger mounting with each failed attempt to break free as he exited the car and tried pulling uselessly on the body and bumper. Sweat dripped down his forehead, flowing through lines of angst that covered his face as his eyes darted around the barren surroundings.

Amidst his exasperation, movement caught his attention from the corner of his eye—a figure shrouded by the shadows emerging from the depths of the swamp woods. The man's presence seemed peculiar, almost unnatural, in that forsaken place. An uneasy feeling spread through L.J.'s overheating body, but desperation outweighed caution. He needed help, and that stranger might be his only chance.

Ankle-deep in mud, L.J. staggered forward, his cries slicing through the stagnant air. "Hey! Wait! Please, help me!" he called out, his voice carrying a mix of desperation and hope. "Do you speak English?" *Stupid.*

The man, barefooted and bare-chested, in oversized overalls, briefly turned. His face remained dark and obscured almost intentionally by the shade before he resumed his journey back into the jungle-like terrain. Ignoring L.J.'s pleas, he vanished deeper into the murky depths, leaving L.J. with nothing more than the whisper of the wind as he struggled to keep up with the stranger, trudging through the sticky mire. Each step was a labored effort against the oppressive atmosphere that seemed to thicken as he ventured farther. The sky dimmed as if the sun itself had relented to the encroaching darkness.

A foreboding silence settled upon the swamp, punctuated only by the distant croak of a hidden creature and L.J.'s grunts of effort. The air grew heavier with the scent of decay, and the echo of distant whispers increased. L.J.'s heart raced as he realized the magnitude of the situation were he to get lost. The weight of the unknown pressed against his sanity as a strangeness assaulted his senses he could not describe.

The murky waters of the swamp seemed to breathe, emanating an energy that enveloped him. Panic ensued, tightening its relentless grip on his chest, and he turned to escape the haunting nightmare.

But as L.J. pivoted to retreat, he stumbled on a protruding root. He fell, and before him, a cottonmouth water moccasin snake coiled, its malevolent eyes gleaming with a sinister hunger. It hissed, revealing fangs as sharp as daggers, glistening with deadly poison.

To evade the serpent's wrath, L.J. rolled to his side, but fate conspired against him. The ground gave way beneath his weight, and he plummeted into a nest teeming with writhing serpents. The snakes struck, their fangs sinking deep into his flesh, their venom injecting a searing pain that coursed through his veins like liquid fire.

L.J. screamed out in panic and pain, his body aflame. His breath was lost in the dark pit, and he could catch air no better than he could escape.

An army of slithering bodies surrounded and slinked upon him, their relentless bites multiplying his torment. With every agonizing moment, the lines between nightmare and reality blurred, melding into a macabre dance of suffering. He fought against the endless assault to break free from the attacking frenzy of the serpents, but his strength quickly waned, and his body succumbed to the relentless onslaught.

As the venom coursed through his system, L.J.'s vision blurred, and his consciousness fled. The pain subsided, replaced by a cold numbness that enveloped his being. With one last gasp, he let himself sink into the encroaching darkness, collapsing into the depths of the swamp, his cries lost amidst the haunting whispers that echoed through the marshland.

$\sim$

THE MIDDAY SUN bore down upon the hotel pool deck, exhausting a furnace of sweltering heat onto the surrounding streets and buildings. Seeking refuge from the relentless swelter, Gwen and her daughter Jenny lounged by the sparkling pool of a quaint hotel within a tropical garden getaway quietly hidden inside the bustling city.

Gwen settled into a poolside chair, her feet dangling in the cool, rippling water. Jenny sat beside her, legs swinging back and forth as she hesitantly dipped her toes into the inviting blue pool. Despite the heat, the young girl remained uncertain, eyeing the glistening surface with a mixture of trepidation.

"Come on, sweetheart," Gwen encouraged, a warm smile gracing her lips as she glanced at Jenny. "It's scorching out here. The water's perfect. Just like a giant bathtub!"

Jenny wrinkled her nose slightly, her gaze flickering between her mother and the pool. "Daddy said he'd be back soon. Maybe he can come to the hotel and swim with me." Her voice held a hint of disappointment mirrored blatantly in the sagging of her shoulders.

Gwen reached out, placing a comforting hand on Jenny's arm. "I know, darling. Your dad's probably held up with errands. He's got some work to do at the house and will be back before you know it. How about we sit here and chat until then? We can come here again with Daddy sometime."

The mother and daughter sat side by side, the gentle sounds of splashing water and distant laughter filling the air. Gwen engaged Jenny in a conversation about their new life in the city, painting vivid pictures of their future home and the adventures that awaited them.

"I can't wait to make new friends!" Jenny exclaimed, her eyes brightening with enthusiasm.

"I wouldn't mind some new friends, too. I'm kinda excited for a new start. Less drama."

Still, within her own vision and dreams, Jenny shared, "I want to have a tent in my room so Daddy can sleep over until I make friends."

Gwen chuckled softly, brushing a stray lock of hair from Jenny's face. "Always Daddy," she smiled. "That sounds like a wonderful idea, honey. But what about me? Can I sleep over, too?"

Jenny giggled, nodding eagerly. "Of course, you can visit, Mommy! But you should sleep in your room 'cause you'll be tired from planting flowers with me and playing with our new cat or dog."

Gwen's heart swelled with warmth at her daughter's excitement. She pulled Jenny into a tender hug, holding her close for a moment before releasing her. Reaching for her phone, she attempted to call her husband once more, hoping he'd finally pick up.

As the phone rang, Gwen's brows furrowed in concern. She glanced at Jenny, a tinge of worry coloring her features. "Seems like Daddy's phone still isn't going through. Maybe he's stuck in traffic, or his phone's out of battery. We'll try again later, okay?"

Jenny nodded, but Gwen could sense her daughter's disappointment. Worry nagged at Gwen's mind, but she pushed it aside, focusing on making the day memorable for Jenny.

"Hey, how about we plan that flower garden for our new backyard?" Gwen suggested, trying to brighten the mood.

Jenny's face lit up with enthusiasm. "Yes, yes, yes! We can pick out the prettiest flowers together!"

With renewed excitement, the pair spent the afternoon planning their future garden, discussing the vibrant colors and fragrant blooms they wanted to cultivate.

As the sun began its descent, Gwen looked at Jenny, her heart full of love for her daughter. "You know, honey, even if we don't see Daddy today, we can still make the most of our day together."

Jenny nodded, a small smile gracing her lips. "Yeah, we'll have so much fun."

Gwen dialed L.J.'s number once more, hearing nothing but his voicemail. She sighed, slipping her phone back into her bag.

"I'll bet Daddy is on his own little adventure that he'll tell us all about when we get back. Maybe we shouldn't give him such a hard time about the hunting. He needs outlets like that, for whatever reason. I think after Daddy got sick, he's had a hard time getting things back into his control," Gwen said softly, trying to mask her deeper concern with a suspicion he may just be sulking.

Jenny looked up at her mother, a hint of worry in her eyes. "He'll come back, won't he, Mommy?"

Gwen embraced Jenny, holding her close. "Of course, sweetheart. Daddy will always come back."

"Were you friends with Daddy when you were little?"

Gwen pressed a finger to her lips, contemplating opening a door to the past. "I was friends with your daddy in college."

"How did you meet him?" Jenny took a contemplative slurp from her smoothie.

Gwen did the same with her beverage. "I was at a bar, and the friend I was with at the time wasn't being so nice to me."

Jenny turned her head, tilted with slight concern. "Was it a boy or a girl?"

"It was a boy."

Jenny shrugged. "What did he do?"

"Daddy or the other boy?"

Jenny pressed her own pensive finger to her lips, a mirrored trait from her mother. "The boy first. Then Daddy."

"Well, the other boy grabbed my arm and tried to pull me. I didn't want to go. Your daddy came up and tried to be nice first, then punched the other boy right in the nose."

Jenny smiled. "He was like your knight in shining armor."

Gwen looked at her phone again, biting her lip. "Let's enjoy our time together, okay? C'mon. I'll get in the water, too, and we'll call Daddy again to see if he wants to take a break in the pool."

Jenny beamed.

As the evening descended upon the hotel pool, mother and daughter remained intertwined in a warm embrace, cherishing the moments they'd shared and plans for their new future, hopeful for the return of the missing piece of their family puzzle.

4

The world wavered between reality and an otherworldly realm. Blue sweat dripped down L.J.'s forehead, mingling with the black blood oozing from the snake bites that covered his body, but it was he who watched himself from above.

In his delirium, L.J. found himself standing at the threshold of a dilapidated cabin nestled deep within the swamp's heart. The air hummed as he was beckoned inside by a mysterious figure cloaked in shadows. Candles flickered ominously, casting dancing shadows upon the walls adorned with curious symbols and ancient artifacts. Smoke spiraled upward from a blazing fire, its acrid scent mingling with the sharp tang of burning herbs. The fire was in a pit, confined by walls of a home, but the roof was gone. L.J., again, found himself looking in from above. The witch's chants reverberated through the chamber, a haunting melody that seemed to pierce L.J.'s very soul. He was placed on a rough-hewn table, and the witch's hands moved with purpose, applying salves made from rare botanicals onto his wounds.

The room pulsated with an unearthly glow as the fire crackled and the smoke swirled around him. L.J.'s vision blurred, his consciousness drifting in and out like a leaf caught in a turbulent stream. He could see the witch's eyes glowing with a spiritual intensity, seemingly peering into the depths of his being. Reality and hallucination intertwined, blurring the boundaries of his perception.

As the ritual reached its crescendo, L.J.'s awareness flickered like a dying ember. The chanting, the smoke, the fire—all merged into a phantasmagoric cyclone that engulfed his senses. He felt himself slipping away, teetering on the precipice of consciousness and oblivion.

L.J. awoke with a pounding headache. His vision blurred as he tried to make sense of his whereabouts. He found himself in a decaying mobile trailer, the walls adorned with peeling wallpaper and the same swampy, musty scent that clung to his skin, hanging heavy in the air. Confusion etched deep lines across his face as he struggled to recall how he ended up in this forsaken place on a padded bench doubling as a bed.

As his senses and recollection sharpened, L.J. noticed the overalled stranger he'd seen before, hunched over a stopgap stove, brewing what L.J. had recently learned was chicory coffee. The pungent aroma wafted through the air, mingling with the scent of bourbon, cutting through the musk filling the room. L.J.'s gaze fixed upon the stranger's weathered face, etched with wrinkles and a dark complexion that he could have mistaken for shadow. The man's clothes hung loosely on his frame, tattered and ill-fitting.

Summoning the courage to speak, L.J. introduced himself, hoping to establish some semblance of familiarity. But the stranger remained silent, his gaze locked on L.J., eyes the color of yellowed fall leaves bearing witness to a lifetime of hardships.

Finally, the stranger spoke, his voice gravelly and tinged with a touch of menace.

"You almost died out there," he rasped, his words punctuated by a solemn tone. "Shouldn't a followed. Something doesn't want you in these parts. Or doesn't want you to leave. You need to rest for at least another six to eight hours. She gave you Wolfsbane. Toxins slow the heart, so venom doesn't flow fast. Usually upsets the stomach, but her herb mix'll fix that."

L.J. recoiled. His heart still seemed to pound in his chest. Questions swirled in his mind, but before he could voice them, the stranger continued.

"Aiyana. Aiyana Martin. She's a root doctor. Folks in the city say she's a swamp witch, but we pay no mind out here. Locals know she's part Creole, part Choctaw. Few of Choctaw Nation left around these parts. Some Houma still around." He spoke plainly as though he was saying anything L.J. would understand. "She lives at the crossroads, as she calls it. Place where all roads depart. Where she can see all corners of the world. People from these parts bring her their sick and their dead. The dead are alive to her. I wasn't sure which one you were."

The older man settled into his worn armchair, his gaze distant. L.J. listened intently, his wounds somehow healed but still pockmarked with the memory of the snake's venom. The room seemed to hold its breath as the old man spoke, his voice carrying the weight of ages past.

"She mixes old Indian ways and Hoodoo in her root cure," the old man began. L.J. could've sworn the windows shook with his words. "When all those serpents sank their fangs into your flesh, it appeared death had come knocking at your door. But fate has other plans. Those plans have been written—largely by your own hand. Destiny."

"I don't understand. How is this possible? I hardly have a scratch. I vaguely remember, but thought it was a dream."

The man leaned forward, his gnarled hands finding solace in each other. "In these parts, we turn to Hoodoo for remedies that science cannot comprehend. The root doctors have the knowledge of forgotten ancient herbs and rituals passed down through generations, each with its own sacred purpose. This one draws from family ties in many of these land's memories. Good and bad."

The old man's eyes sparkled with reverence as he described the intricate process. "To cure snake bites, the root doctor seeks specific herbs. The life-giving plantain, the gentle shepherd's purse, and the powerful yarrow. Each herb holds within it the essence of healing and protection."

A smile tugged at the old man's weathered face as he continued. "The root doctor makes what she calls a poultice. She crushes the herbs into a batter-like paste mixed with clay from the mound and her spit, and puts that right on the bite to suck out the venom and ease the pain. You may not see it, but you'll still feel it. That's for sure."

L.J. leaned closer, captivated by the tale of ancient wisdom. "A bunch of plants and spit saved me?" He winced, feeling the residual pain. He ran a hand absentmindedly over the space where the wounds once were.

"It's not just that," the old man warned. "She guides the healing process with a sacred ritual. Burns bundles of sage and sweetgrass. She uses the smoke to purify the air and ward off evil spirits. The spirits lingered long around you. They want something or know something."

His voice dropped to a hushed tone, revealing the gravity of the next step. "Aiyana recites a bunch of incantations, whispered in ancient tongues, and calls upon spirits of the land and her ancestors for their divine intervention. It is their energy, their power, that seals the bond between the land's herbs and your wounded flesh."

The old man's eyes met L.J.'s, filled with compassion and reverence.

"You were fortunate, my friend," the old man breathed. "She recognized the urgency and acted swiftly. Her hands were guided by forces we cannot fully comprehend. She wants to give you a chance— a chance to test the true mettle of the man you are."

L.J. nodded, gratitude etched upon his face like a name upon a tombstone. The old man's words carried a weight that resonated deep within his soul. He understood the concept of tradition and ancient practices that bridged the gap between the seen and unseen, though he had no time for such musings wasted on fantasy.

"Shit! I need to call my wife. Holy shit, I'm so fucked." L.J.

searched his body, then looked around the small confines to see if his phone had been removed and placed somewhere while he recovered. "It's gone. Shit. Shit! Maybe it's in my car."

"You won't find any reception for a phone out here, anyway. I don't own one," the stranger said with a hint of disdain. "There are no neighbors for half a mile, and they don't have phones either."

A dense sense of isolation settled over L.J., along with the realization that something trapped him in this desolate place with no means of contacting the outside world. He yearned to call his wife to assure her of his safety, but the stranger's words extinguished that hope.

"I need to leave. Need to get back." He tried to elevate himself, but stars collided in his head, and his limbs faltered. "This was a mistake. You need to drive me home. I'll pay you. Whatever it takes."

Curiosity piqued, the stranger leaned closer, his eyes gleaming with an intensity that sent L.J.'s heart into a flutter. "Why are you out here, not knowing the area?" he inquired, voice laden with curiosity and caution. "Bad enough you come out here. You could have gone all the way down to Bayou Sale Road. That'll get you in some real trouble."

L.J. hesitated, then divulged his purpose, sharing the tale of his search for a big game hunter, driven by his desperate need for a bear and a black wolf.

The stranger's ears perked, a flicker of interest on his wrinkled face.

"You've heard of the black wolf?" L.J. questioned.

A sly smile curled upon the stranger's lips. "Call me Lon. If you're serious about the hunt, I can get you out in the woods tonight. It will be a full moon, and with luck, you might get a good kill shot."

L.J. couldn't believe what he was hearing. The story seemed too fantastical to be true, yet Lon's unwavering conviction left little room for doubt. "Is it dangerous?" L.J. asked, his voice tinged with fear and excitement. "And, legal? Like—screw it. Really, it's true, and you can take me?"

Lon's amber yellow eyes bored into L.J.'s soul, his voice dropping to a near-whisper. "The black wolf is like no other. It carries a curse, and its howl pierces the night like a wounded banshee and the devil himself. Some who have seen it claim it stands on two legs, a twisted hybrid of man and beast. But one thing's for certain—it's a monster of a hunt. Get some sleep, L.J., and I'll wake you at sundown. You'll see your family soon enough. The spirits have confirmed it."

5

L.J. stirred from another uneasy slumber on the vinyl leather RV bench. His heart raced from remnants of haunting nightmares concerning snakes, wolves, and walls painted with blood. As his eyes adjusted to the dimly lit room, he noticed Lon meticulously filing the tips of bullets, hunched over his desk made from an old discarded console T.V. fitting, as he loaded the cartridges into a high-powered rifle clip. Intrigued, L.J. craned his neck closer, examining one of the gleaming bullets. His voice laced with curiosity and a hint of humor, he remarked, "Is that silver? You didn't say we were hunting werewolves, Lon."

The lighthearted smile on his face faded when the old man's darkened eyes met L.J.'s. He remained silent, allowing the weight of his gaze to convey the severity of their endeavor.

L.J.'s jest fell away, replaced by a growing sense of anticipation and trepidation. That, paired with the matter of his disappearance, weighed heavily on his chest and caused his fingers to fidget and flicker with anxiety. Under normal circumstances, a stupid move like this could've been the break in their already crumbling marriage. But L.J. knew he'd just uprooted Gwen from friends and family; there wasn't much turning back with all the bragging she'd dropped before their departure. He braced for sleeping on the couch or in the guest room for at least a week or two. He thought of Jenny, and her opinion of him and hunting and how he missed her and how she once smiled at him and took his hand and how they made pancakes together and how he taught her to ride a bike.

Lon gestured for L.J. to listen closely, snapping him back to the present.

"Here's what's going to happen, kid. You sure you're up for this?" L.J. nodded, unsure whether it was to affirm his readiness or simply to bring himself the courage he thought he needed. "Sure you don't care how it could impact your life?"

L.J. shrugged. "In for a penny, in for a dollar. There's no turning back. Guys in the swamp boat shop asked the same thing. I realize I'm just a guy from Chicago asking to hunt their local game, so I'll just say I appreciate the opportunity and know what I'm getting into. I've taken down some pretty enormous creatures—got a giraffe once on a retired zoo game range in Montana. Let me tell you. Those guys are *big*. This one time, in Montana, I baited a cougar with a dead rabbit. Shot the big cat...fucking huge, I might add... and put the rabbit in its crossed arms like it was a stuffed animal during nap time. Oh, shit, I got a lot of laugh replies on that one. LOLs all day long. You know. Like Instagram hands up, fire, all that shit." L.J. beamed and antici-pated a response of approval. "Impact? Hell yeah."

Lon's face turned sinister, any hint of concern no longer lingering in his eyes.

"Be that as it may. I won't go against the spirits. All signs are here, signaling that you're the perfect one." Lon continued, "I'm going to give you a head start. I want you to hike up about a mile along the path behind this trailer. The ground will rise to a mound, an indigenous burial mound of sorts—local Choctaw call the place their second passageway. I want you to climb it until you stand at the very top. From there, you'll see the black wolf coming toward you." As L.J.'s eyes widened, Lon's face threatened to break into a smug smile. "He won't be able to get up that mound. You'll be safe. Take the shot. But don't leave the mound until the black wolf is good and dead. You've got three shots of these special rounds and three more standard rounds in case you come across something else on your way out. I'm leaving one more of the silver ones here in the trailer in case something goes bad." His voice dipped low. "Hunts like this, something always goes bad."

"Have faith in me. Not my first rodeo, Lon," he said, arrogance glowing.

"Yeah, you said that." Lon huffed. "I was you until recently. Trust me. I've learned more about this world in the last hundred days than an entire population can learn in their lifetime."

L.J. voiced a question, but Lon silenced him with a raised hand, his expression shifting to one of determination. "Don't worry about me," he said, his voice resolute. "This is your hunt. You need to face the black wolf alone. A man like you will never stop. Clearly, it's your nature, possibly your bloodline, your very DNA, knowing it has to come back home. I'll decoy, then flush him out to you."

The gravity of Lon's words settled upon L.J., mingling with the thrill of the impending hunt and solidifying a rightful place. His mind raced with questions, and he couldn't help but ask, "How much do I owe you? What happens if I get caught? What if there are other hunters?"

Lon's response was quick and assured, his eyes locked with L.J.'s. "There won't be anyone else out tonight, kid. As for payment, your word will suffice. Don't tell anyone about this for at least a year. If you make the kill, you'll be doing more for me and this area than you can imagine. Sure you can do it?"

L.J.'s breath caught in his throat as he absorbed the weight of the agreement. The magnitude of the hunt was both thrilling and daunting, and he knew he had to prove himself as he thought back to all the locals who'd dismissed him as though he was nothing more than a tourist. With a firm nod, he affirmed his commitment once more, knowing he'd be posting about the kill on social media as soon as he grabbed his phone from the Range Rover. There was no way he was going to pay the price with Gwen if he didn't win the internet for the day.

Lon's face cracked into a wry smile, his eyes lightened to a near glow, and his complexion darkened.

"Then run," he urged. "Run as fast as you can. And don't look back until you've faced the black wolf and emerged victorious. You can be the one to actually end this."

With those parting words, L.J. took in a deep breath. The air charged with anticipation, he bolted out of the trailer into the inky night weapon in hand, any lingering pain left behind. Lon watched him go, his gaze lingering in the darkness as if imparting a silent blessing upon the young hunter and one for himself.

The hunt began, and as L.J.'s footsteps echoed through the night, he knew that this encounter with the black wolf would be a test of courage, skill, and unwavering resolve. He'd been hiking through silent marshland for what he supposed was about ten minutes when the sky erupted with a dreadful, fear-inducing sound. A blood-curdling howl came from behind.

"Oh, shit. He said, run. But he didn't say from the fucking wolf. Lon!"

L.J.'s heart pounded, sending pulses into his ears. The rapid thud drowned out the sounds of his labored breaths as he sprinted through the treacherous swamp woods of the Louisiana bayou. Fear gripped him, squeezing tight on his ribcage as he pushed his weary body to its limits. The relentless pursuit of the ravaging wolf echoed behind him, it's snarls and howls reverberating through the moonlit foliage.

Every step was a struggle. L.J.'s legs soon turned heavy and unco-ordinated, hindered by the murky swamp water and tangled under-growth. Panic gnawed at his senses as his eyes desperately flitted over the surroundings, searching for any sign that he was still on the right path. Doubt slid into his mind like the venomous serpents that had ravaged him, questioning whether he was running toward safety or straight into the jaws of danger.

With each passing moment, his fears multiplied. Images of lurking alligators and enraged wild boars filled his mind, their primal instincts sharpened by the moon's eerie glow. The beams of cold blue light twisted the undergrowth into gnarled shapes that his mind turned into ravenous, unfeeling beasts stalking him. The thought of more venomous snakes slithering beneath the murky waters and hidden within the shadows only intensified his dread, and every reed that trailed over his legs reminded him of the danger. *What the hell was I thinking?*

The wolf's relentless pursuit intensified, it's howls echoing through the night, a chilling forecast of impending doom.

L.J.'s ears strained to discern any other sounds that might betray the presence of the wolf's pack, if it had one, growls and snarls weaving into the fabric of his terror. He no longer knew if what he was hearing was real or part of the fantasy hunt.

Just when despair threatened to consume him, hope flickered like a distant candle in the darkness. Through the moonlight's ethereal glow, he caught sight of a majestic silhouette—the crest of a large hill. The old burial mound, his sanctuary, lay a hundred yards ahead.

Adrenaline surged through L.J.'s veins, pushing him to new heights of endurance. The hill became his singular focus, a beacon of safety beckoning him forward. His strides lengthened, fear and fatigue temporarily forgotten, replaced by sheer determination as he used the weapon stock for balance and leverage.

As L.J. closed the distance, the sounds of pursuit became louder, the wolf's menacing growls reverberating through the night air.

The hill loomed larger; its form more defined with every breathless stride.

He could almost taste the relief, the promise of respite from the relentless chase, but the wolf's fierce determination mirrored his own, its presence a constant reminder that escape wasn't assured.

Finally, with an ultimate surge of effort, L.J. reached the foot of the mound.

His legs burned, his chest heaved, but his resolve remained unyielding.

He cast a glance over his shoulder, the wolf's glowing eyes piercing the darkness.

"Oh. Shit. Oh, shit. You're big. You can't... get... me... on... the hill. I hope."

Summoning every ounce of courage, L.J. propelled himself up the steep incline, his hand clawing and rifle stabilizing him along the uneven earth, tearing up clumps of the sacred ground. His body protested, muscles screaming, but he pressed on, fueled by sheer willpower and the trill of the hunt.

At last, he reached the crest of the burial mound, his body collapsing against the hardened ground. He clung to the earth, gasping for breath, his heart thundering in his ears.

The wolf's menacing howl echoed through the night, but it had become a distant cry, fading into the wilderness and dissipating amongst the reeds.

L.J. lay there, his exhausted body trembling with relief and lingering fear.

The battle was not yet won, but in that moment, as he gazed up at the moon, he found solace, knowing that he had made it one step closer to survival.

He was sure the wolf had not left the area and would search for a way up the hill.

L.J. pushed himself up, his eyes scanning the gloomy expanse before him. Sure enough, the wolf was there, just as Lon said it would be.

The beast, even in the shadows, was huge, unlike any prize L.J. could have imagined. It reared from four legs to two and back again, paws thudding against the sodden earth.

"Let's go, buddy," L.J. coaxed himself. "Let's make this worth the shit you're in." He raised the weapon to his shoulder and peered through the scope.

He slid his finger to the trigger and heard snorting sounds coming from his rear—short, forceful exhales that burst with nervous huffs and guttural growls.

L.J. froze.

6

L.J. brought himself to a rapid stand atop the hill, his heart rate elevating to a level never experienced and his legs melting into Jell-O as he found himself amid a perilous predicament. To his left, the fierce wolf prowled along the mound's rim, its piercing yellow eyes fixed upon him with an intense hunger that he knew only his flesh could satisfy. To his right, a massive black bear emerged from the shadows, its towering presence exuding power and dominance.

Every instinct in L.J.'s body screamed at him to run. His muscles tightened, ready to escape the imminent danger closing in on both sides. But L.J. saw himself as a seasoned hunter who had faced countless trials in the semi-wild. Flight was not an option. Survival hinged upon his ability to remain composed and think swiftly and strategically amidst the chaos.

L.J. kept his gaze fixed upon the majestic alpha. Sweat trickled down his forehead, but he clenched his jaw, refusing to show weakness. The wolf's eyes locked with his as if challenging him to make the first move.

Meanwhile, the black bear, a formidable force of nature, pawed at the ground, its mighty frame blocking any escape route L.J.'s eyes sought.

The ground trembled with each step it took, causing nearby trees and bushes to quiver.

L.J.'s hands tightened around his weapon, his fingers finding solace in the familiarity of a rifle stock. He knew his only chance was to hold his ground and display his prowess as the apex predator.

With calculated precision, L.J. raised his weapon. His senses sharpened. He watched the wolf's movements, the way it stalked closer, testing his mettle. Turning, he assessed the bear, noticing its gradual advance, an unyielding force of nature fueled by instinct.

"Well, look at you, L.J.," he said to himself with a grin. "The man said no one will be out tonight. Wolf will just circle but can't get you. Bear is ready to charge up this hill. It's a no-brainer, silver bullets or not. This is a double-money moment. Bear wins the silver, wolf gets lead."

L.J. fired at the black bear, dropping the large beast to the ground, but only for a moment.

The bear howled in pain but got back to its feet and charged up the hill. "Shit!"

L.J. chambered another round and shot again.

The bear kept coming.

He shot a third time.

The bear dropped.

The ground underfoot shuddered as it landed. Trees trembled, their leaves rustling with the intensity of an angry crowd.

The black wolf rose to two feet and broke through the binding circle, charging up the sacred mount with a howl that couldn't be distinguished between a raging man or the mound itself screaming in protest, "No!"

7

L.J. dropped to a defensive squat atop the desolate hill. The wind raged through the trees as cloud cover shielded the only source of light, and darkness descended upon the land. He clutched the hunting rifle with white-knuckled fingers, knowing that his life depended on the three precious shots that remained.

The massive black wolf charged toward L.J., its eyes burning with a feral hunger. Its vicious growl grew louder and more menacing until it filled the air like a roaring river of terror that obscured the howling wind.

L.J.'s finger trembling on the trigger. He stood and took aim, trying to steady his shaking hands.

With a thunderous blast, the first shot erupted from the barrel, ripping through the sounds of the night.

But the wolf, undeterred despite a brief slowing upon impact, continued its relentless advance.

L.J. fired his second shot in quick succession; it made a desperate crack through the dense atmosphere.

The creature stumbled, its pace faltering for a moment, but it regained its footing, baring its sharp fangs with a menacing snarl before continuing its approach.

L.J.'s heart sank as he realized he only had one bullet left. He took a deep breath, his hands slick with sweat, and aimed with desolate precision. The beast sprung, clearing the last few feet between them with one giant leap.

The last shot pierced the air, finding its mark on the wolf's chest just as the beast launched upon him.

A deafening silence followed, broken only by the agonized groan of the dying beast and the muffled exhaustion of L.J. from underneath.

As the black wolf lay lifeless upon him, a dull pain seared through L.J.'s shoulder. Looking down, he saw blood soaking his shirt, blooming from a deep wound where the creature's teeth had found its mark. His breath caught in his throat, and his head flopped back to the ground as he clutched his injured limb, heaving the beast off him and rolling it to the side.

But his anguish grew deeper when he witnessed an astonishing sight.

The wolf's form trembled. Small shudders flowed through the beast's carcass, and audible cracks, pops, and snaps reverberated across the landscape as the creature's legs straightened and strained. From the wolf's crown, the skull split, and the hide tore as the dead wolf birthed a new convulsing form from within. A patch of hair and rounded head squeezed forth, its nose and jaw flopping from loose contorting flesh. The snout lined with razor-sharp teeth broke away into pieces. Before L.J.'s horrified eyes, the animal pelt slid away in a riptide of blood and mucus as a man emerged from within.

It was Lon, laying naked, covered in a bloody aftermath of his own ignition.

L.J.'s voice trembled with confusion and disbelief. "Lon? How— how is this possible?"

Lon's eyelids opened, the color blazing with fury and anguish. "You fool! It was me all along! The curse, the beast—it was my burden to release as a sacrifice, but you, you wasted the silver bullets on a bear! You were supposed to end it, to free me, to break the chain! You have no idea what you've done. The price you'll pay."

L.J. struggled to comprehend the enormity of the revelation. His words came out jumbled and spluttering. "I didn't know, Lon! I thought you were just hunting the bear or something. I didn't know it was you!"

"You've killed yourself with your greed. I tried to stop you. They all did. I gave you what you wanted in a way that wouldn't kill more. You deserve what's coming. You took what wasn't yours to take." Lon's face twisted with anger, his voice dripping with bitterness as L.J. tried to explain how he hadn't known once more. "Ignorance is no excuse! Because of your error, the curse is now yours to carry." He grabbed the savior-turned-condemned by the collar. "You will hunt down your family, driven by the scent of their blood; once they have died by your hand, you, too, will transform into the protector of the swamps."

L.J.'s mind reeled with horror; his body wracked with pain from the bleeding bite wound. "No... no, this can't be happening." Hands flew to hair. "I won't become a monster! I'd never do that. I wouldn't hurt my family. I *won't* do that."

Lon's voice grew colder, his gaze unyielding. "You have no choice, L.J. The curse demands payment. For a hundred days, you will roam these swamps as the beast, hunting those who threaten the balance of nature, taking from it only what you will use out of necessity, never greed. After, you'll have paid your price. You'll be free to return to life as you know it, if you can live with yourself. No one can."

They both heard a growing whisper in the rising wind. *You must return what you have taken. Give where you have gotten.*

"Do you hear that?" L.J. asked. "Is that real?"

"It's the spirits."

"What do they want?"

"If you had only killed me, you would've been righteous. But you took the bear, a sacred and protected bear. So, the protection of the spirits from this mound opened the path. I couldn't stop it. Now, you have to pay the price."

"By becoming a wolf? This is insanity."

Lon's breathing became less ragged, the words coming easier with each one he spoke. "They call it the Rougarou in these parts. All the original locals know its curse. It's far worse than insanity. Before your first change, you'll be driven to hunt your own; the smell of their flesh and blood will take over. They can't run, can't hide. It's neither man nor wolf. It's a supernatural abomination that brings out the devil's wickedness of both."

"No way. Never."

Lon rose to his feet as if he'd only had the wind knocked out of him from a tackle. "You can't help it. Nothing you can do. All that's left is to follow the paths the spirits take you on. They'll take you back to where it all begins and, for many, where it ends. You can stay in the trailer. If you can live with yourself, the curse will be gone after the time has passed, then, you transfer it to another who has done an injustice to the land. It's the penitence for us all. Now come on."

"No. No. I have to go. I need to get home."

L.J. looked for the dead bear. Astonished, he saw the last remnants of it absorbed by the mound, skin melting away, then muscle, before the bones were pulled into the earth by the grass.

"This was your hunt, L.J. And for all you've screwed up, you're doing one last thing."

"No. No fucking way. I'm outta here."

The warning growl from Lon caused L.J. to step back and reconsider his plan.

～

WHEN THE TWO made it back to the trailer, Lon instructed L.J. to wait. The naked man went inside and then returned with a bottle of whiskey. "Give me the rifle."

L.J. did as asked. "Where are you headed? Do I have to come?"

Lon chambered the silver bullet from his pocket and headed off toward another trail.

"Wait, I don't really have to come, right?"

"Yeah, L.J., you do. I need to take you to the first homestead. To the circle."

"But I—"

"Shut the fuck up for once. Not everything is about you, as you'll soon learn."

They walked about five hundred yards to a clearing. There stood the remains of an old log cabin, roof caved in, walls collapsed.

There was an impression in the earth. What little moon could shine through the cloud cover showed a one to two-foot-deep depression ten to twelve feet wide.

"Stay outside the rim."

L.J. stepped back. "What is this?"

"Here. Take a swig."

"I'm good, Lon. No, thanks."

"I'm not asking you, L.J. I'm telling you."

L.J. swallowed a bit until Lon held the bottle to his mouth, forcing more down L.J.'s gullet.

Lon took it back once satisfied and spilled the whiskey in the center of the mound. He raised the bottle to L.J. before taking his own long pour. Lon smiled at L.J. and licked his lips. "See ya in Hell, kid. I'm sorry about what you're going to do. All I can say is before you leave them tonight, take something of theirs that's silver. You're gonna need it. Accept the wolf as your brother. Life must eat life. You took life. Now you'll eat from your life that you must give as the first sacrifice." Lon flipped the rifle under his chin, barrel pushed into the soft flesh beneath his jaw, reached for the trigger with his thumb, and fired.

The night exploded, and a pink mist briefly peppered the night's hazy light. Lon crumpled to the ground, dead.

"Oh, my god. Oh, my god."

From the echo of the gunshot replied sounds of the swamp. Soon, calls of the night drew closer and closer.

Take, and you must give, it repeated in an eerie almost-whisper. *L.J. wasn't sure whether the voices were in his head or riding on the wind.*

He fled down the path, looking back to see creatures great and small entering the circle to feed on the remains of Lon. The earth soaked up the flowing blood from his split skull.

When L.J. spotted his vehicle, he did not stop, not even when he arrived at the Range Rover. L.J. continued running, legs strong and lungs full, feeding his bloodstream with the spirits of the swamp air.

"No, no," he pleaded to himself, unable to stop the word from flooding his mouth. "No!" he screamed as he ran, guided by an internal compass toward home, following an instinct, chasing a scent carried to him by the spirit world of the bayou.

8

"Mommy, I miss Daddy. Can we go home?"

It was all Gwen needed to hear before relenting with the ease of blowing out a candle. L.J. was going to pay for this disappearing act, but nonetheless, she grabbed their things as the nightlife crowd was picking up in the French Quarter. In less than thirty minutes, the Uber pulled up their drive to a home with the house lights off.

"Is Daddy home?"

"I don't see his car, honey."

"Let me try his phone again."

Voicemail.

"Goddammit, Lair! Where the hell are you?"

Gwen flipped to the Life360 tracker app. "I still don't see... wait, a light just turned on in the house. He's home. And baby, if Mommy gets a little loud and angry, it's only because I'm being communicative. I still love your daddy, but he's in hot shit if things aren't done."

"Yay!" Jenny scrambled from the car, running to the house.

Gwen, slow to follow, gathered their things and headed up the drive, only to see the lights flick off again. "Okay, someone turn the lights back on, please," she called. "Jenny?"

Gwen strolled along the side of the house in a shifting gait of slow and fast until she climbed the back stairs. The gravel scraping underneath her feet made her cringe unconsciously, her body attuned to each noise she uttered.

She came to a harsh stop upon seeing the wood of the door frame splintered, the knob hanging at an awkward angle.

"Jenny!" Gwen dropped her bags and sprinted into the house and through the kitchen, screaming for her child. She weaved through a warren of stacked boxes, cursing her husband as she tried to peer over them, knocking several over to find her daughter.

At the grand staircase, Jenny stood in the dark, her slight frame silhouetted by the scant moonlight coming through the glass of the front door and front room windows.

"Jenny, come on. Let's go outside. I think someone tried to break in."

"Mommy," Jenny said, pointing to a dark corner.

"What is it?" Gwen asked, raising a foot to step closer but immediately sensing better and sliding back, her daughter drawn closer.

"Larry? Larry, is that you? Are you drunk? What the fu—"

A low whimper was uttered from the corner. "Please. It's not safe here. Go back to the hotel." L.J. stood in the shadows, shoulders hunched awkwardly and hands clawed into the walls. "Go. Run! Please!"

"Daddy, are you okay?" Jenny broke free and rushed to her father.

"Someone turn on the goddamn lights," Gwen ordered before Jenny screamed.

~

As a wire-haired terrier, Max couldn't tell the time, but every night, like clockwork, he needed a 10:30 p.m. stroll. He wagged his tail happily on that night like every other as he bounced down the sidewalk, his leash pulled taut in Sarah's grip. They walked in relative silence, interrupted only by the faint rustling of leaves and the occasional distant car passing by.

When they approached the new neighbor's house, a sudden flicker of light caught Sarah's attention. She turned her gaze toward the otherwise darkened house and the faint glow emanating from within.

It also distracted Max. Ears perked and nose in the air, he was rooted to the spot. Whether it was curiosity or concern that compelled Sarah to halt in her tracks, it was the same for Max. Her heart quickened, and she strained her eyes to focus on what was happening through the dimly lit windows. It was the muffled scream she heard first and then Max barking, which continued as long as the screaming. Sarah's breath caught in her throat as she witnessed the most horrific sight unfolding before her.

In the shadows of the house, the silhouette of the man remained ever-present. He moved swiftly from room to room, confused, enraged, monstrous. The man's actions were frantic, his movements quick and merciless. It was as if a deranged beast had been unleashed, hell-bent on causing harm to the... two—the family? The helpless figures. Their desperate cries for mercy echoed through the brick walls and into the night. The sheer brutality of the scene froze Sarah in place, her body trembling with fear and impotent rage.

Tears welled in her eyes as she desperately grappled for a way to help, but she was a mere spectator, powerless in the face of the unfolding tragedy. Her grip on Max's leash tightened as her mind raced, torn between staying to bear witness and seeking aid.

Time seemed to slow to a crawl as the relentless assault continued, never-ending. The weight of helplessness pressed upon her, suffocating her spirit. She yearned to intervene, to protect the innocent, but fear rooted her to the spot, an invisible barrier between her and the violence consuming the dark house that the fists of her humanity pounded against.

The night remained in mournful silence, save for the sound of shattering glass. It was a macabre ballet of evil played out within the walls of that forsaken house.

As the last lit window darkened with the shadow of the enormous figure peering out to the streets, the bitter truth settled upon Sarah's shoulders: the nightmare was over; the violence had been swallowed by the blackness within. She stood there, drenched in terror, sadness, and guilt. She had been a spectator to the unthinkable, a witness to unspeakable horror, and yet, could do nothing but pray for the victims' safety until Sarah realized it was her, he was looking at.

Sarah turned away from the house in fear of her own life. As she spun, ready for flight, it was then that she noticed the other neighbors standing across the street behind her, equally alarmed by the horrifying scene. Some of their faces glowed as they captured videos on their phones. Others must have dialed 911. The night and lives in the Garden District of New Orleans were shattered.

Within moments, police cars raced through the streets, sirens blaring, their red and blue lights flicking shadows of the surrounding crowd onto the scene.

As the police vehicles skidded to a halt outside the distressed property, an officer spotted two neighbors weeping on the sidewalk, as he exited the car, their faces etched with terror. The officer called out, glancing at their tear-streaked faces. "What happened here? We received reports of screams and an attack."

Eyes, bloodshot and haunted, looked up at the officer. "We... we heard the screams, saw a man attacking a woman... and he... he threw —I think it was a child. Then he, well, he—I can't even say it."

The officer's brow furrowed, sensing the magnitude of the situation. "Do you know the people involved? Are they your neighbors?"

"They—they just moved in. We don't even know their names."

"I do," one spoke up. "Talbot."

The officer exchanged a glance with a sheriff who had also arrived on the scene and heard the name as he approached.

The sheriff, a man with a knowing look in his eyes, raised an eyebrow. "L.J. Talbot, you say?"

Surprised, the officer turned his attention to the sheriff. "You know him, Marcus? What's the connection?"

Sheriff Marcus Gaudet's gaze shifted upward, his eyes fixating on the full moon in the night sky. "We tried to stop him," he sighed. "There was no way we were going to stop him. Met him the other day. He was looking for a hunting guide. Wanted to take down some big game."

The officer's curiosity piqued, but a sense of unease quickly settled over him. "Hunting what, dare I ask?"

The sheriff's expression grew grim, reality carving deeper into his sun-beaten face. "He seemed awfully intent on finding that wolf, almost driven. We've seen that look before; it never bodes well."

The police officer removed his hat, running a hand through his thinning hair. "God forgive him if he found what he was looking for. God forgive them," he said, turning to the house. Neither of them rushed to the scene.

The sheriff nodded solemnly. "Let's go inside and find out. Something tells me this is exactly what we know it to be."

As they stepped through the threshold of the house, a wave of a repugnant stench washed over them, causing both the officer and the sheriff to gag involuntarily. Their eyes widened in horror as they surveyed the macabre scene before them.

The sheriff and the officer, their faces pale and ashen, staggered out, desperately trying to keep their stomachs from heaving. It was a scene of unspeakable violence and carnage. They would've thought the walls were painted red had it not been for a glimpse of white at the very top that betrayed their true nature.

The sheriff and the police officer shared sorrowed eyes. The full weight of the situation was dawning on them like a new heartfelt day in The Big Easy. Something primal, something dark and untamed, had been unleashed again.

They stepped outside together. Silently, standing side by side, their eyes fixed on the moon, as if seeking guidance or protection from the ominous night sky. In the depths of their souls, they knew the hunt had just begun, and the horrors they were about to face were as timeless as the legend.

~

L.J.'s breath came in ragged gasps as he sprinted along the shadows of the urban terrain's concrete jungle, then through the rural under-brush, his footsteps soon pounding against the forest floor. The familiar rhythm of his gait shifted, some unyielding force urging his body to surrender to its metamorphosis. He fought against the encroaching change, but his muscles quivered, aching to be released.

He tumbled and clawed at the ground to find purchase, keeping up with an inner drive that his prior form could not sustain. Rounded fingernails tore and pulled from their beds each time he fell to the ground in agonizing transformation. His skin sloughed away as a new form was born.

As he struggled to run, L.J.'s strides grew longer and more force-ful, his legs stretching and coiling with an unnatural strength, tearing through his flesh. His body hunched forward, spine arching as a shudder of agony coursed through his being while skin shredded to make way for a wet and bloodied hide. His hands, once outstretched for balance, curled and twisted into primal claws. Again, he fell and rolled. Again, he rose amidst the torture and trauma, flesh dragging behind him like a snakeskin.

The bones within him cracked and rearranged, reshaping with each insufferable step. The colostomy bag fell to the ground as his intestine stoma grew outward and fell off his body, forgotten beneath morphing feet. They elongated, the toes merging. Stout pads forced themselves through his blistering flesh. Shoes and clothing, similarly, fell away, ripped to shreds. His legs bent at an unnatural angle, muscles bulging with newfound power. The surrounding trees seemed to shrink as his once upright posture contorted into a preda-tory crouch.

And then, in an instant, L.J.'s transformation reached its peak.

The physical pain that had consumed him transformed into a surge of wild energy. His memories and mental anguish fell away to make space for a new primal focus. The horrific recollections remained in a compartmentalized but accessible corner of his mind, pushed back by the irresistible allure of his inner beast. With a guttural growl that resonated deep within his chest, L.J. surrendered himself to the call of the curse.

His body propelled forward, but instead of bounding on two legs, he raced through the forest on all fours. His arms and legs moved in unison, powerful limbs thrusting him with astonishing speed. The once-human man had become a creature of the night, the Rougarou. His primal instincts guided his every movement.

As L.J. sprinted through the dense thicket, his senses heightened to a supernatural degree. The earthy scents of the forest filled his nostrils, and he became aware of every part of the world surrounding him; the rustling of leaves, the croaking of frogs, and the distant hoot of an owl resonated within his sensitive ears. His eyes, glowing with an eerie luminescence, pierced through the darkness, enabling him to navigate the nocturnal world with uncanny precision.

He bounded effortlessly through the obstacles he'd previously blundered through, his body flowing with grace and power. Each leap covered a great distance, his form a blur as he weaved through the trees. The wilderness embraced him and the unleashed might of his lupine form. It assured him that now was his time to give back nature's spirits regardless of what sorrow lingered.

Through the moonlit forest, the man-turned-wolf raced, his presence a testament to the ancient forces dwelling within him. He had become a creature of feral beauty and relentless strength, a being at once feared and respected in the supernatural realm. Tonight's hunt and sacrifice, the first. The next was already assaulting his senses and coming into sight.

9

A storm fast approached the Garden District as if it, too, wanted to wash away the bloodbath. Rain cascaded down, its steady rhythm matching the somber mood that engulfed Detective Labatte and Sheriff Gaudet. They stood before the house, its usually cheery facade marred by darkness and despair. Yellow police tape fluttered in the wind. Inside, the remnants of a horrifying act awaited their formal investigation.

Jack, a tall and weathered detective with a five o'clock shadow that perpetually adorned his hardened face, took a prolonged drag from his cigarette, the smoke interrupted by raindrops, as he headed to the door. It didn't take but a few steps before he exhaled slowly, eyes narrowing as they surveyed the gruesome scene before him. The room was drenched in blood, shattered furniture, and glass. The lifeless bodies of a woman and young girl lay sprawled across the floors, their once vibrant lives extinguished by an untamed savagery and laid to witness along the hardwood.

"Looks like a goddamn massacre, Marcus," Jack muttered, his voice heavy with disgust and pity. "Only the cycle of the beast could've done this."

Sheriff Gaudet, a burly man with a thick Southern drawl and steely resolve, nodded in agreement. His eyes scanned the room, taking in the grisly details that told a tale of unfathomable violence. "We all know this ain't human work. There's only one state of rage that would cause someone to tear another apart with bare hands. Hundred and one days. Dale, Beau and a couple other boys confirmed it earlier."

Jack flicked the cigarette butt into a nearby puddle, the flame sputtering out. He pulled out his notebook, already forming a plan. "We need to write this up in the usual way. One that won't raise eyebrows," he said, his voice low and deliberate. "People come here for vampires, werewolves, and witches, but they aren't ready for the reality of it all. We'll use the same old story of the killer being on drugs, you know, PCP or something. Or, I dunno, he had a psychological episode, a temporary madness. This guy was from Chicago; did social media stuff. Dig up dirt or throw dirt on him."

Marcus rubbed his weary eyes, considering Jack's words. "Yeah, that'll work. We'll say the husband isn't a suspect right now. He's missing; we'll hint that he might be a victim himself, but we'll also suggest it could be one of those unsolved serial killings that happen around the area. That way, folks won't suspect anything out of the ordinary. Locals will just know it happened again. Old families know exactly what happens. Especially if they find out he's got Thibadeau blood."

"Guess that settles that." Jack's tone was tired.

As they huddled together, rain trickling down their collars, the detective and the sheriff began crafting a narrative, weaving a tale of human darkness to shield the truth of the supernatural world lurking just beyond the shadows. They knew that the public's belief was fragile, easily shattered by the weight of the unknown and any skepticism it brought.

Sheriff Gaudet straightened his hat, determination etched upon his face. "I'll go take a look at that old RV in the morning," he declared. "It's where they always go before they inevitably come back to the city or blow their brains out. I'm sure we'll get calls in the morning of some roadkill having been dragged for miles. Maybe I'll try this guy out and see if he can help take care of our other problems. Lon was a pretty fit partner." The sheriff kicked at the ground. "His wife used to babysit me once upon a time."

"Sorry, Marcus." Jack patted his shoulder, a flicker of knowingness glinting in his tired eyes. "Gator season's starting up. Means poachers. If this guy gets a hold of 'em, we'll have more missing persons. And we already know something's going on in there that wasn't Lon."

Marcus nodded.

They may have been dancing on the precipice of reality and myth, but together, they would write a story that would pacify the skeptics and keep the whispers of everything supernatural at bay. In the world they inhabited, the darkness often wore the disguise of the everyday, and it was their duty to confront it, even if it meant bending the truth. However, something else had been terrorizing the swamps, and they'd let the locals just think it was the Rougarou. A few horrible known things were still better than the unknown.

With the rain still pouring down, the duo stepped away from the eerie crime scene, their resolve firm. They would venture into the abyss and fight the monsters that lurked within, armed with little more than a pen and a tale as twisted as the truth it concealed.

≈

L.J. stood at the edge of the deep swamp. His heart, now with more pulmonary veins and a greater heart rate, aided his heavy breath. Heavy but not labored. He was not the least bit tired. The lights of New Orleans had long faded behind him, replaced by the impenetrable darkness of the wilderness. His memory, once a tapestry of human experiences, now hung in tatters, replaced by primal instincts.

In the velvety blackness of the night, his vision ignited, leaving every detail of the surrounding swamp laid bare before him with vivid clarity. His eyes, once human, glowed with an eerie yellow hue, reflecting the predatory intensity within. Shadows danced and twisted around him, concealing the myriad creatures that called this place their home.

His sense of smell, heightened beyond his comprehension, allowed him to dissect the intricate tapestry of scents that permeated the air. With each inhalation, he could taste the musk of the swamp, the damp earth, and the life teeming within. His nostrils flared as he surveyed his surroundings, able to detect the scent of almost every animal within his vicinity.

Then, through his sprint, his gaze fell upon a small deer, its body hunched and limping, the survivor of a brutal alligator attack. Its future, sealed by nature's cruel design, marked it as prey, destined it to succumb to the relentless circle of life. The deer's weakness called out to L.J., and the primal hunger coursing through his veins.

Silently, he stalked through the dense undergrowth, every step calculated, every muscle primed for the hunt. The deer's labored breaths echoed in his ears, it's scent intoxicating as he approached. The anticipation coiled within him, ready to spring forth in a savage dash.

As the distance between them dwindled, L.J.'s instincts took over completely. Without warning, he lunged, teeth and claws sinking into the deer's vulnerable flesh. A rush of warm blood flooded his mouth. The animal's futile struggle against the inevitable fueled the fire of his feral hunger, driving his fangs deeper into the savage ecstasy of the kill. He tore, ripped, and delved deeper.

As he tore into the carcass, wild sounds of approval pierced the night. The growls of coyotes echoed in the distance, their predatory chorus drawing closer with each passing moment. Their presence alerted L.J. to the threat they posed, but in short order, they surrounded him and his feast.

Their heads hung low, tails between their legs. A couple lay

before him in complete submission. L.J. backed away from his kill
with his belly full, allowing the pack to gorge on his leftovers.

He turned his head to a sound he should have been alerted to
sooner but had been drowned out by the praise of his underlings. His
eyes met the piercing yellow gaze of an immense alligator, its
bellowing snarl revealing rows of bone-crushing teeth. The behe-
moth approached, its movements swift and cautious.

But L.J. refused to cower. In that moment, he was the embodiment
of wildness and ferocity. He stood tall, his own snarl fierce and
unyielding. The clashing sounds that reverberated through the
swamp warned of a predator standoff.

The massive alligator, sensing L.J.'s dominance, slunk back,
acknowledging the primeval force that stood before it as its protector.

In that confrontation, the boundaries between human and
animal blurred. L.J. had become a creature without conscience. And
as the swamp whispered its secrets in the night, the lingering question hung heavy in the air—how would he ever find his way back to
the realm of man? Was he forever condemned to roam the primordial
realm, a killer and beast among beasts?

10

The transformation from wolf back to man could have been painful, but the last hours were fuzzy, so it was merely his body that remembered. The memories were vivid, but he wasn't sure they were his own. L.J. sat alone in the dimly lit confines of the RV he had come to claim, the silent morning interrupted by the occasional drip of water from a leaky faucet that led to an electrical well pump. The inside of his new abode long held a stench of blood and decay he hadn't fully noticed before, a grim reminder of the horrors that had unfolded the night before and evidently decades before that.

The clothes he found were ill-fitting but covered his bare skin well enough. He pulled his hands through the sleeves, raw and caked with dried blood and the underlying transformation mucus and ruptured vessels and cells, evidence of the unspeakable act he had committed. The vague and distorted memories continued to float through his mind like specters, tormenting him with flashes of violence and terror that only came when he felt most vulnerable. He knew what he'd done and struggled with how and why he couldn't stop himself with sheer rationality.

His head throbbed with a dull ache as he strained to piece the events together. Images danced at the edges of his consciousness— his wife's terrified face, his daughter's innocent gaze, and then darkness. Something had taken hold of him, a force beyond comprehension. It had unleashed a rage that consumed him, leaving behind only the wreckage of his shattered family.

Agony gnawed at his soul, the weight of his actions crushing him with guilt and despair. He clutched at his temples as if physically trying to squeeze the truth out of his tormented mind. "What have I done?" he whispered to himself, his voice a hollow echo in the stillness of the RV.

Every fiber of his being screamed for an explanation, for some way to rationalize it, to make sense of the unspeakable. But there was none. L.J. was trapped within a hell of his own making, lost in the murky depths of his fractured psyche. The more he fought to understand, the deeper he sank into his abyss of guilt.

The RV, once a brief sanctuary at the start of his dream adventure, had come to feel like a tomb. The walls closed in around him, suffocating him with their silent accusation. He stumbled to his feet, his movements unsteady and slow. Pain coursed through his body, a physical manifestation of the torment that continued to alter his body.

L.J. staggered toward the small kitchenette, his gaze falling upon a photograph that lay abandoned on the counter. It was a silver-framed snapshot of someone's happier times, a wife, daughters, and sons smiling, blissfully unaware of the darkness that likely awaited them. His trembling hands reached out, tracing the contours of their faces, a feeble attempt to connect with the symbol of the love he'd destroyed.

Tears welled in his eyes, blurring the image before him.

As the morning light seeped through the curtains, casting long shadows across the RV, L.J. sank to his knees, his anguished cries filling the confined space.

Until he had a thought.

The root doctor.

◠

THE FAINT HUM of cicadas filled the humid air as the sun began its descent. L.J. remained with his grief inside the cramped trailer all morning and afternoon. He had thought solitude would be his only companion until he dared to seek the healer, but the approaching sirens shattered that illusion.

L.J.'s heart leaped as two police cruisers pulled up outside, their blue and red lights flashing, sirens silenced, as they rolled their vehicles toward some shade. L.J. knew exactly why they'd come. He had prepared himself for the moment, ready to face the consequences of his unimaginable crime. How they knew where to find him wasn't even a distant concern.

Taking a deep breath, he stepped out of the trailer, hands raised high above his head, surrendering to his fate, face tilted to the ground. The officers, clad in their authoritative uniforms, emerged from their vehicles, guns holstered at their sides. But to L.J.'s astonishment, they did not immediately move to apprehend him.

"Put your hands down, L.J.," the sheriff called out, his voice laced with an unexpected calmness.

Confusion flickered across L.J.'s face as he hesitantly lowered his hands, eyes darting between the sheriff and the officer beside him. "I... I don't understand. You're not here to arrest me?"

The other officer, a seasoned man with a grizzled beard, stepped forward. His eyes, weary from years policing the swamp, bore into L.J.'s soul. "No, son. We know what you've done. Sheriff told me of your encounter the other day. We know you're responsible for the deaths of your family. We also know how things work out here. You're subject to a different justice now."

L.J. struggled to comprehend the words that hung in the air. "Different justice? What do you mean?"

The Sheriff stepped forward, placing a firm hand on L.J.'s shoulder. "Kid, this swamp has its own set of rules, its own brand of justice. For generations, the people who lived here have been bound by an ancient pact with nature. Your ancestral family was part of that. And you, my friend, have become a part of that pact. To say you fucked up is an understatement," his hand weighed a little heavier on L.J.'s shoulder, "but you fucked up your own self and your own family. Our job is to keep you contained and focused in areas where you can make a difference."

L.J.'s mind spun with disbelief. "What are you saying? I'm supposed to work for you now?" Something triggered within L.J., an instant rage. "You knew. You knew this would happen. You could've stopped me! You could've saved them!" L.J. lunged at the sheriff, but he'd been in that spot before. He pivoted, pulled his weapon, and hammered the back of L.J.'s head.

The officer dropped his boot down on the back of L.J.'s neck. "You made your choice like every other man. Right now, you're just a man. At night, when the moon hangs high, you transform into that creature with strength beyond measure. That transformation comes at a price. You must use that power to help us, to protect the swamp from the criminals and miscreants that seek refuge here. The spirits have their use for you, and so do we. We like to call that a balance of nature."

"Just kill me. Kill me." L.J. gritted his teeth as his head was pressed to the ground.

"Not how it works, boy," the sheriff said. "Don't make your family die in vain. Make something of yourself. Make something out of their memory."

A mixture of anxiety and intrigue flooded L.J.'s veins. The weight of his guilt mingled with a new purpose, a purpose he hadn't expected. "And if I refuse?"

The officers exchanged a knowing glance. "Most folks worry only about the coon-ass Cajuns. But poaching here takes food out of our hands and right from our family's mouths. It's a declaration of war against the people here. It also violates the laws of the swamp. The swamp will enact its own form of justice. The darkness will consume you, and you'll be forever lost within its unforgiving depths. And there will come a time when your curse has been paid, and you'll either blow your own brains out in the sacred circle, or we'll make you wish you had. Understood?"

The officer lifted his foot.

L.J., slow to get up, stared into all that was the swamp and the mysterious allure that pulled him deeper into the unknown. The officers' words echoed in his mind, the weight of centuries pressing upon his shoulders. "And if my life is meaningless at that point, which it will be, why should I care?"

The officer shrugged. "You'll have a period of self-loathing, but even that has its limits. We'll make sure you get hooked on the needle so you can be a good boy on the street, sleeping in your own filth with the rest of the strung-out pack."

With a hesitant nod, L.J. accepted his twisted fate. "If this is the way of the swamp, then so be it. But don't think I'll ever forget what I've done."

The gray-bearded officer placed a hand on L.J.'s shoulder, a gesture of understanding and unexpected compassion. "We don't expect you to forget, son. We expect you to carry that burden with you, to remind you of the horrors that can unfold when one loses oneself in this darkness and the darkness of their heart. I warned you. Nothing but your own selfishness took what you had. You're paying the price. For that, we're square."

As the sun dipped below the horizon, the officers became fidgety. "We'll be in touch. For now, you let your instincts lead you. That's the spirits. But so help you, if you resist and head into the city, you'll find a new hell to pay."

L.J. nodded.

"Oh, and L.J., be careful. You may not be the only beast hunting in the bayou."

11

As the lawmen had said, once the moon rose high in the ink-black sky, casting a ghostly pallor over the still waters of the murky bayou, the hunt was on. Two figures, masked by shadows, silently maneuvered their small boat through the obscure channels. Their intentions were far from noble. Poachers, thieves of the swamp's natural treasures.

Clad in dark, weathered clothing, their faces were hidden beneath camouflaged neck gaiters. Quietly, they paddled the narrow waterways. With stealthy precision, they approached the hook-baited alligator fishing lines that had been meticulously set hours before by the legal tag owners, unaware of the trespassers lurking beyond their eyeline.

One by one, the poachers methodically cut the lines and thundered their headshots into the thrashing beasts' skulls before removing the prized reptiles from the waters and rightful owners. The moonlight glinted off the gun barrels, an ominous reflection of their illicit activities. The swamp itself held its breath, awaiting retribution from its champion.

They hauled several other writhing alligators toward their boat, and the creatures fought in desperation against their captors. The sound of splashing and jaws snapping echoed through the night, blending with the chill of the bayou's calls. But amidst the chaos, the poachers' intuition sensed a looming presence. An unsettling feeling prickled the hairs on their necks. They doubted their solitude, for they knew the legend but were tempted to challenge it.

Unease settled over them like a creeping fog as unseen eyes followed their every move. Whispers carried on the wind, the ethereal voices of long-forgotten spirits, warning them of the impending doom that awaited their transgressions. Yet, their greed pushed them further into the heart of darkness.

The silence wavered. A low, feral growl reverberated through the night, resonating from the waters to the boat's bottom.

The surface of the surrounding water trembled, ripples spreading toward them like an ominous prelude to their reckoning, their movement no longer the only thing responsible for the water's disturbance.

"Nick, keep an eye out dat way," one of the poachers whispered.

His buddy nodded and pointed to a rustling bush by the shore.

Both rose their weapons to the direction of movement.

The leaves shook.

Nick retrieved a high-lumen flashlight from his pocket and flicked the switch.

The bright beam caught the reflective eyes watching the men.

The creature moved from the light as their rifle barrels remained trained on every hint of movement.

Fingers at the ready, a fat swamp water raccoon emerged as if in surrender. It waddled from the underbrush, staring at the men and squinting at the blinding light before it, too, was distracted by a new movement in the surrounding brush.

In an instant, a massive creature lunged from the depths of the bayou's darkness, eyes like hellfire. Its hulking form crashed onto the boat, sending the stolen alligators and poachers alike into a scramble of flailing chaos and panic.

Guttural screams pierced the night as the creature's gnashing jaws tore through flesh and broke bones, its savagery a testament to the wrath of the swamp itself. Limbs flailed, blood mixed with water in the boat's bottom, and desperate pleas for mercy were lost in the onslaught of violence.

The moonlight, stained crimson, was appeased with the gruesome fate of the poachers, and shone even brighter on their remains. Their cries diminished, soon replaced by the distant cries of nocturnal creatures whose mournful howls blended with the moans of the swamp's approval.

The beast remained in the rocking boat, feasting on the dead men. L.J. ripped muscle and tendons with his teeth, pawing at the meat, holding tight to ligaments and bone. He slurped the life that burst from fountains of arterial rupture.

The bayou reclaimed its stolen bounty, and the waters slowly settled, hiding the remnants of the poachers' fate beneath its dark surface. The creature, sated and satisfied, soon melted back into the shadows, leaving nothing but a chilling presence behind and the promise of no mercy or escape.

∼

L.J., his senses heightened from his recent kill, followed a flickering campfire glow that danced in the distance. His hind paws sunk into the marshy ground, mud squelching between his toes as he traversed the bayou, his keen eyes scanning the surroundings for any signs of danger or opportunity. The sight that awaited him, however, was far from what he had expected. His nose poked through the air, taking in a fresh, sweet scent of a woman.

In the clearing, bathed in the eerie glow of the fire, a figure swayed and twirled, her silhouette casting elongated shadows upon the surrounding trees. Long dark hair trailed her movements, light in the air as it danced around her.

L.J. closed the distance quietly, his raging spirit calming.

Figures crafted of twigs surrounded the woman's enclave. Broken skulls of beasts adorned the trees in a protective perimeter.

The root doctor swamp witch, L.J. thought to himself as his rational mind returned. He watched with enchanted intrigue as she held the sides of a multicolored, free-flowing dress in front of her as though it were her dance partner. She emanated an aura of intimate connection to the mystical forces that governed the bayou, drawing L.J. to her just as he had been drawn to the backwater. As she continued her dance, perhaps a solemn ceremony, her voice carried whispers of ancient incantations through the humid air.

Intrigued and drawn by the allure of the witch's ritual, L.J. continued his approach with a deep sense of trust, his body gradually peeling, twisting, and cracking from its lupine form back to that of a man. As he emerged from the darkness, his presence no longer cloaked in fur and fangs, Aiyana Martin turned her gaze toward him, a knowing smile playing upon her lips at the bloodied naked man seeking answers, as they all did.

"Welcome, L.J. The spirits told me you would soon join us," the witch's voice carried an ethereal resonance as if it reverberated through the very fabric of the swamp itself before coalescing in his ears. "Come closer. I have sensed your turmoil, your desire for release from the curse that plagues you. I'm pleased you survived the bite from the poison vine, but know it was you who stepped on Brother Viper. I offered them a prayer for forgiveness, and they accepted. Let me help you again."

Hope blossomed within L.J.'s heart as he took hesitant steps forward, his eyes fixed upon the enigmatic figure before him. "Can you even help me? I don't want to hurt anyone else." He sobbed. "I didn't know. I couldn't stop it."

The witch's eyes glittered with ancient wisdom; her voice filled with a hint of sorrow. "Oh, dear L.J., I possess the power to heal, to create curses, to weave the threads of fate, but to unravel the curse of the Rougarou is beyond my reach." She extended an arm. Whether she was trying to grasp the curse or his arm, L.J. couldn't tell. "The powers of nature have deemed it so; you must endure the weight of your actions."

Despair etched itself onto L.J.'s face as he pleaded with the witch, his voice tinged with a fragile mix of hope and anguish. "But there must be something; some other way to atone for what happened." His acceptance of the deed grew less personal with every cycle of the wolf's blood circulating through his body. Still, his human side emerged periodically in flashes of overwhelming emotion.

The witch's gaze softened, a flicker of compassion crossing her features. She extended a hand, palm up, offering solace in her words and the wrinkle of each fingertip. "L.J., redemption lies not in the lifting of the curse but in how you navigate its consequences. The path of the Rougarou is one of vigilance and protection. Find purpose in your affliction. Let it guide you to balance the scales of nature."

A deep, weary sigh escaped L.J.'s lips as he considered the witch's words, the weight of his past actions whipping to the forefront of his mind and resting heavily upon his soul. Acceptance mingled with the extinguished embers of his hope, and he nodded solemnly. "I understand."

The witch's eyes gleamed with approval as she raised her hand, invoking the power of the swamp. "Go forth; may the spirits of the bayou guide you. Embrace your transformation, for it is both your burden and your resolution. The path of the Rougarou shall be yours to walk, a penance for the deeds that haunt your past, and a gift for your future to know the world in its truest form."

"I need to get them back. It wasn't me. That can't be it. I can't move on from this."

"Most men do not, and some never learn from their ways, pining for their return to the wolf." Aiyana reached down and picked up a stone. "One hundred and one nights you will spend. Each day, when you awake and are no longer the dark soul eater—the *Nalusa Falaya,* as my mother's people would call the beast—put a rock at the base of the mound where you were bitten. It connects my ancestors to another mound of life, *Nane Chaha, a* mound that had a path to the center of the Earth before man's existence. From the waters came the mud. From the caverns arose all things living."

As she handed him the stone, she said, "It connects to the place where the first sun blessed all things and where man followed my people from the hole and killed nature's children as they emerged. If you please the spirits, perhaps *Aba*, the good spirit, will return to you what was lost. To give you back life once you, yourself, have become reborn. Tomorrow will be your first true test as you return to the mound, to your second birth, to win back what was yours as you follow a trail of death and tears of your own creation."

With her last words hanging in the air, the witch resumed her dance, her form melding with the shadows of the night. L.J. stood for a moment.

In the depths of the bayou, where darkness and mysticism entwined, he embraced his destiny and felt the coarse hairs and wolf form labor to re-emerge as he crossed the threshold of Aiyana's domain.

12

And so, the nights passed. L.J. continued on the prowl, his lupine senses acutely attuned to the sounds and scents of the Louisiana swamps. Even when out of sight, the moon in all shapes and forms awoke him, calling his shift forward. The lives of men were stolen like their own unsanctioned kills, and the wounded, deformed, and suffering creatures of the forest were given mercy and returned to the ground. This was now L.J.'s territory, and he moved through it with grace, each step a testament to his untamed power and the forgiveness he hoped to achieve as he placed each morning's stone.

The forest had always been his sanctuary, where he could embrace some hidden desire, but it had turned to exploitation and mockery. All reverence had fallen to his ego around the time his father had passed on, and his mother left her only child for another man. The start of the pain and helplessness he once carried. He had come to embrace and relish the freedom that came with his lycanthropic nature, the way he could move through the wilderness with an uncanny beauty and a predatory cunning. The confidence it gave him. For once, he felt like a true alpha. Power. Control. That night, though, there was something different in the air, a sense of unease that set his hackles on edge. *This is new.* His fur bristled. The unfamiliar scent irritated his innate senses. His confidence wavered ever slightly.

As he ventured deeper into the swamp, he picked up on strange noises carried by the night breeze: the rhythmic creaking of a boat and the hushed whispers of men conspiring in the dark. His keen ears perked up, and he followed the sounds until he reached a small hidden inlet.

There, illuminated by the faint glow of a lantern, he found two men huddled in a rickety boat, their faces obscured by wide-brimmed hats and dark jackets. Thick fingers tugged at abandoned fishing lines, snatching alligators from the murky waters, a dangerous and illegal activity in those parts once the season had come and gone. L.J. couldn't help but feel a surge of anger; the hunters were testing the natural balance of the swamp with the same irreverence he, too, had possessed.

Still, something was off.

Just as he was contemplating whether to confront them before they made their kills, a series of shots rang out through the night. The loud, sharp cracks of gunfire echoed among the trees, and L.J. instinctively dropped low to the ground, his senses on high alert and his muzzle pressed into the earth. From his vantage point, he watched in shock as a man stepped out of the shadows, his face a mask of grim determination. The intruder set his rifle down in the grass and retrieved a gleaming hatchet that reflected the moonlight just as the waters did.

L.J., even as a beast, felt a flicker of intimidation as he caught the sinister glint in the man's eyes as he approached the poachers.

Taken by surprise, they struggled to respond. One of them raised a shotgun, but the intruder was too quick. With a swift, brutal slash of his hatchet, he disarmed the poacher and slashed again in a vicious arc that left the man writhing on the boat's wooden planks. A dismembered hand dropped to the boat's bottom with a heavy thud.

The other poacher reached for his own weapon, but it was too late. The intruder lunged forward, his hatchet finding its mark, and the man fell with a brief gurgled cry as his neck was split.

L.J. watched in horror as the intruder showed no mercy, no remorse. He finished the poachers with a cold efficiency that sent shockwaves down L.J.'s spine. Blood stained the boat, and the two lifeless bodies lay motionless, their eyes staring vacantly into the night sky.

The intruder wasted no time. Within minutes, he'd ransacked the boat, plundering weapons, wallets, and any valuables the poachers had in their possession. With a cruel twist of his lips, he tossed their bodies into the water, and watched them sink with satisfaction. The boat, stripped of its cargo, was dragged into the dark waters, disappearing beneath the surface with a trail of bubbling pops.

As L.J. crouched in the shadows, he was torn between the desire to approach the ruthless killer and the instinct to protect his own existence. The murderer's actions were brutal, but something in the way he moved, the cold calculation of each movement, continued to send fear throughout L.J.

The intruder moved with quiet confidence through the swamp, guided by an innate sense of direction and purpose as L.J. followed him. His path in the darkness was meandering, as if he knew the area well, and L.J., even in wolf form, was hard-pressed to keep up. The dense underbrush and murky waters seemed to pose no obstacle to the man as he ventured deeper into the swamp.

After a while, L.J. saw he was heading toward a small clearing. The faint glow of a campfire pierced the night, painting the surrounding trees in swaths of flickering light. L.J. hid behind a tree, watching as the intruder stepped into the clearing. He crouched by the fire, studying the stolen wallets and weapons.

The man was a mystery. His face was obscured by a scruffy beard, and his clothes were worn and stained. Despite his unassuming appearance, L.J. couldn't shake the feeling that there was more to the stranger than met the eye.

As the intruder settled by the fire, L.J.'s wolf-like ears picked up the sound of muttered words. The man was talking to himself, his voice low and raspy. L.J. strained to hear, but the words were too soft to make out. He inched closer, creeping silently through the shadows and tall grass until he was within earshot.

"...They had it coming," the intruder muttered, his voice tinged with a bitter edge. "Stealing from these waters, ruining what's left of the bayou."

L.J. couldn't help but be taken aback by the man's words. *Sure, the poachers were breaking the law, but did their actions warrant such a brutal response?* He knew the bayou was a fragile ecosystem, and poaching could do irreparable harm, but murder was a heavy-handed solution, at least from a man not cursed to do so. After all, L.J. had no choice. He was driven to murder by an uncontrollable instinct. *It was the beast, right?*

The intruder glanced around the clearing; his gaze distant as if lost in thought. "Sometimes you have to be the wolf among the sheep," he murmured, his eyes flickering with an unsettling intensity that made his onlooker think twice about approaching. "It's a cruel world out here, and we've learned that the hard way."

L.J. was torn. He couldn't let the man's actions go unpunished, but he also couldn't ignore the danger emanating from the stranger. There was something dark and foreboding about him, something that demanded treating the situation with caution.

The intruder finished his grim contemplation, rose to his feet, and tossed one last glance at the scattered loot. Then, he moved toward a small tent nestled in the shadows at the edge of the clearing. L.J. seized the opportunity and silently trailed behind him.

The man stopped and lifted his head high, moving slowly.

Can he see? What is he looking for?

L.J. witnessed the man's nostrils flare.

Smell.

The man lowered his head and continued on.

As the intruder entered the tent, L.J. positioned himself just outside the opening, hidden in the darkness. He watched as the man settled down, the light of the fire still casting a soft, flickering glow on the tent fabric. The man's breathing grew slow and steady, and it was clear he intended to rest for the night.

L.J. knew he needed to gather more information before making a move. He was determined to uncover the truth about the enigmatic figure who had crossed his path and why he had resorted to such extreme measures. The moon still perched high in the sky, and the swamps continued to share more secrets, but one thing was certain—the night was far from over, and the swamp was no longer the sanctuary L.J. thought it was.

13

No matter how long a person lived in the bayou, the swamps remained an eerie and treacherous place. The murky waters shimmered like liquid silver, pulling on the gnarled and twisted shadows dropped by branches and trees, distorting and reshaping them in their own image. Amongst the haunting terrain, L.J. moved with instinctive grace, his fur-covered body absorbing the night, welcoming the change with each stride.

In his lupine form, L.J. embraced the DNA of a true bestial hunter of the land where it was kill or be killed night and day. The wind carried messages from the spirits; the rustling leaves whispered new truths to him, and the ever-shifting scents of the swamp told a story only he could decipher. It was both a gift and a curse, and on that night were shared fragments of a story to be revealed as one of blood and terror. L.J. smelled the scent of gasoline, oil, sweat, and fresh-killed game.

With the intruder from the previous night at the back of his mind, for the next few hours, L.J. patrolled his territory, the vast expanse of dense, shadowy swamp that was now his home. It was a world of subtle danger, but he had grown to understand its intricacies as days turned to weeks. It was indeed a place of balance, where life and death existed in a delicate dance, and L.J. was the keeper of that balance, just as other shapeshifters before him who had served their sentences toward atonement.

L.J.'s sharp ears picked up the sound of a struggle. A stifled cry for help sliced through the swamp's living systems before it was cut short. His keen instincts led him toward the source of the commotion, and as he moved closer, the scent of blood and fear filled his nostrils.

Something was terribly wrong.

Following the scent, L.J. crept through the dense underbrush, his eyes locked onto the disturbing scene unfolding before him. Through a thicket of twisted vines, he watched in horror as a man, cloaked in darkness, stood over the lifeless body of another. The victim's barren eyes stared up at the moon.

L.J. crouched low, hidden by the shadows, his heart pounding against his ribcage. He had stumbled upon a murder, a chilling act of violence that was as much a perversion of the swamp's balance as anything else he'd seen.

Reveling in his kill, the figure tilted his head back, revealing the same scruffy beard from the night before.

The killer muttered something under his breath; L.J. would've missed it had it not been so familiar. At the chilling incantation, the lifeless body seemed to respond, and to L.J.'s horror, it began to twitch and convulse. The dead man's limbs moved with a grotesque, unnatural grace as if pulled by some unseen force. It was a macabre dance of death, a summoning of dark powers that defied the laws of nature.

As L.J. watched, paralyzed by the terror of that moment, the killer drew the hatchet from his belt and chanted louder. The words were guttural and ancient, a language not meant for human ears. With each chant, the lifeless body on the ground twitched and jerked, slowly rising to its feet, its eyes vacant and empty, little more than a puppet.

It was then that L.J. realized he needed to act. It wasn't just a murder; it was a perversion of the very essence of life and death. With a deep, harsh growl that sputtered in the back of his throat, he lunged from the shadows, his massive form barreling into the killer and sending the hatchet spiraling into the swampy water. The element of surprise was on his side, and the stranger stumbled backward, momentarily stunned by the attack.

In the ensuing struggle, L.J. used his powerful jaws to clamp down on the killer's wrist, forcing him to release his grip on the lifeless marionette he had raised. The reanimated body collapsed in a grotesque heap; its unnatural existence extinguished.

But the fight was far from over. The killer howled in pain as L.J.'s jaws crushed bone. With a swift kick, the stranger sent L.J. tumbling into the water. The swamp swallowed him for a moment, but he emerged, wet and snarling.

The killer reached for a small pistol hidden beneath his coat and fired. The gunshot echoed through the wetlands, and pain seared through L.J.'s back as it struck him. He yelped in agony, his massive frame crashing face-first into the muck.

The world spun as he struggled to regain his footing, his lupine form wavering as his strength waned, bones warping to human from wolf and back again within minutes. The killer dropped the gun and drew a gleaming silver knife from his belt, his eyes filled with cold, merciless intent. He was closing in on L.J., who tried desperately to rise from the swampy ground.

L.J.'s thoughts raced as he fought against the pain in his rapidly weakening body. He knew that if he transformed back into his human form, he'd have no chance to escape. With every ounce of his remaining strength, he willed the change not to come over him as his wound seared and sizzled.

Slowly, despite his will, the fur and skin receded, his bones shifted, and his human body emerged from the wolf's form. The pain was excruciating, but he couldn't afford to stay prone in his weakened state. As he finally stood on two legs, naked in every sense of the word, fear gripped him as the killer stood just a few yards away. Waiting.

The stranger's eyes widened in delight as he beheld L.J. in his human form, the moonlight bathing him from behind, casting contorted shadows on his face. A cruel smile quickly replaced the surprise. "You can change your skin, but it won't save you," he hissed, glancing down at the scraps of fur discarded in the mud. "I always hated the shed. What a mess."

L.J. had no time to respond. With newfound determination, he turned and sprinted through the swamp, his feet sinking further into the muck with each step. Panic coursed through him as he heard the heavy footsteps of the killer in pursuit, gaining ground.

The swamp offered no refuge despite L.J.'s protection of it. The dense vegetation, tangled roots, and treacherous water only slowed him down, making him an easy target. He had to find a way to escape the relentless hunter who had unleashed powers beyond the realm of reason.

As he ran, so did his thoughts. He needed to reach the edge of the swamp to return to the relative safety of his hidden RV. If he could make it there, he might have a chance to defend himself or call for help.

The moonlight dappled through the trees overhead. His heart pounded, and each breath was a struggle. The pain from the gunshot wound in his back was becoming unbearable, but he couldn't afford to slow down.

Behind him, the killer was relentless, his footsteps growing louder with each passing second. L.J. could hear the sinister laughter that echoed through the swamp as though the landscape itself was taunting him. The killer was reveling in the hunt, finding pleasure in the chase.

Just as L.J. thought he couldn't run any farther, he burst through the dense underbrush and stumbled into a small clearing. The edge of the swamp was in sight, and the dilapidated cabin lay just beyond it. Hope surged through him, but it was quickly replaced by fear as he heard the killer's laughter drawing closer.

With a last burst of energy, L.J. raced ahead. *Almost there.*

But the killer was unrelenting, and L.J. could feel his presence right behind him. Just as he reached the mobile home and scrambled up the rickety steps, a sharp pain pierced his side. He stumbled and fell to the wooden planks, gasping for breath and clutching at the wound.

The killer loomed over him, knife in hand, a sinister grin clawing at his lips. "You put up a good chase, wolf," he sneered, "but it's over."

Desperation welled up as L.J. reached for an old wooden board resting in the grass. With all his remaining strength, he swung it at the killer's legs. The sun-hardened weapon connected, and the killer staggered backward, his grip on the knife loosening.

Seizing the opportunity, L.J. scrambled to his feet and made a final, desperate lunge for the flimsy metal door. He wrenched it open and slammed it shut behind him, locking it just as the killer reached the threshold and placed his hand on the handle.

Inside, the dimly lit enclave felt like a sanctuary. It remained cluttered with relics of the cursed lives, but they provided him with provisional weapons. He grabbed a rusty fire poker used to prop a cabinet up, and clenched it in his hand, his heart racing.

The killer gently knocked on the cabin door, his voice dripping with menace. "You can't hide forever, wolf. I'll enjoy carving you up in there."

L.J. knew he couldn't stay hidden for long. The tin shanty was old and thin, and the door wouldn't hold against a light wind, much less the killer's determination. He needed to escape, to call the sheriff for help, but the pain in his back and side reminded him of his vulnerability.

As he considered his options, the killer's knocking grew more frenzied, and the door creaked under the pressure. L.J. felt his heart sink; he was running out of time. The man outside was relentless and had already shown a horrifying mastery of the dark arts.

With a sudden, bone-shaking crash, the door burst open, and the killer stormed into the cabin. L.J. lunged at him with the poker, but his opponent was quicker. He sidestepped the blow and delivered a savage kick to L.J.'s chest, sending him sprawling across the cabin floor.

Pain radiated through his body, and he knew he couldn't fight the man in such a state. As he struggled to get up, the killer loomed over him, the gleaming silver knife poised for the last blow.

"You put up a good fight, but it's time for it to end," the killer hissed.

With a desperate roar, L.J. tried to roll away, but he wasn't fast enough. The knife descended, and a searing pain tore through his side again, ripping further. His vision blurred as darkness closed in, and he felt his strength slipping away.

The last thing he heard was the killer's triumphant laughter before the world faded to black, and he lost consciousness.

In the swamp's heart, the darkness swallowed the Rougarou named L.J.

14

T he sun was hot and high, sending its blinding light and oppressive heat down into the wilderness, where a small campsite was nestled.

L.J., bound on the damp ground, struggled to breathe, ropes constricting his legs, neck, and hands. His eyes darted around the camp, and his heart pounded in his throat as he tried to make sense of his surroundings. Trepidation gnawed at him, but he couldn't remember how he'd ended up there.

A figure hunched over the modest fire, L.J.'s rusty poker in his hand, and a perverse look on his twisted face. He was a man, a sinister embodiment of evil who clearly found his delight in the darkest corners of the swamp. L.J. gathered that he may have been what the lawmen spoke of, striking terror into the hearts of those who dared to venture into his domain. He was a monster in his own right, a predator who had made that forsaken land his hunting ground.

L.J.'s heart sank into the depths of his stomach as he realized he was trapped in the lair of a sadistic murderer. Panic washed over him, and he tugged at his restraints, desperate to free himself. The rope bit into his flesh and held firm. He tried to scream, but the cloth gag muffled his anguish.

The swamp butcher turned his attention away from the fire, his dark eyes locking onto L.J. as he discarded the poker to the fire. He held the wickedly sharp knife in one hand and grinned menacingly as he approached his captive. The blade glinted in the sunlight, a deadly promise of what was to come.

"Awake at last, huh?" The man's voice was a throaty growl, like that of a beast. He leaned in closer, his cold, malicious eyes fixed on L.J. "You know, I've been waiting for you, L.J. Been waiting for you to change back. It's not every day I get to catch a real-life *loup garou*. The spirits called you by name."

L.J.'s heart raced, and he struggled to find his voice. Never in his wildest imaginings did he think he'd be the one to fall into the clutches of another madman in the swamps. He regarded the haggard-looking stranger in the fire's light. His head was deformed; half of it was missing. Something had caved or crushed the skull on one side, and jagged scars ran the length of the separated hairline and scalp.

"You don't know what you're dealing with," L.J. croaked. "I'm not a monster like you. I was cursed."

The man chuckled; the sound curdled L.J.'s mixed blood. "Cursed, huh? Everyone's got a sob story, don't they? Mine's just a little different. I kill people now, not animals. It took hundreds of years, but I've had enough of the beasts in this swamp."

L.J.'s mind raced as he considered his options. The ropes binding him were too tight, and the man was too close. The sun was far from the horizon, and darkness wouldn't envelop the campsite any time soon. The change wasn't coming. He was far from a ravenous, blood-thirsty monster. He was just a bound, helpless man.

"Listen, you don't understand," L.J. pleaded, desperation clear in his eyes. "When I change, I won't be able to control myself. I'll become a killer, just like you. You don't want this. Let me go, and I promise I'll never return."

The killer sneered, his knife glinting ominously in the firelight. "You think I'm afraid of you? I've been waiting for this moment. You're the weakest one yet. I want to see you become the ultimate predator, just like me." The man looked down at his bitten arm when he noticed L.J. staring at it. "I guess Lon didn't pass on the message. The spirits don't want to give me the power again. I've had to take what I can from the witches, the dead, and the damned."

"If you know what I am, you know what I can do," L.J. threatened.

The man laughed. "Listen to the alpha taunt. Are you the alpha, L.J.? Are you stronger than your relatives who blew their own brains out after the passing? I did once, too." The man patted his head then walked closer to the fire. "I got lucky. I learned what it meant to be king. To rule." The man turned the hot poker, then raised it, showing the tip that glowed yellow, orange, and red. "Silver bullet to a non-vital. Ouch. Silver knife to a non-vital. Ouch. We're just starting to have some fun, L.J." The man leveled the poker to L.J.'s head, then swiftly sent the hot iron into L.J.'s wounds.

L.J. screamed.

The man lowered the prod to where L.J.'s stoma bag once hung, the orifice lightly healed over, and sent the hot metal through the skin.

L.J. howled in agony.

"No worries. It will heal the next time you transform. Oh, wait," he almost giggled, "you can't. Your journey is done. You've passed the curse on. How does freedom feel?"

"No," he choked out. "No. I'm not finished. I need more stones."

"Ha! Did you really think they would bring your family back? Oh, they all fall for it." The stranger twirled the rod casually, the tip skimming dangerously close to L.J.'s nose. "That's the only way the spirits get you out of your misery. Smart. They never gave me that option. I was the first. I had to figure it all out."

"I'll kill you," L.J. mustered through the scorching pain.

The man dropped the poker with a thud and a hiss as the heat boiled the moisture in the grass.

"Are you the alpha, L.J.?" He bent down, twisting his body as he crouched.

"Yes, I'm the alpha." L.J. gritted his teeth. "I'm the alpha of the swamp."

"Really?" The killer unfastened his belt buckle, standing. Next, the button of his pants was undone, and the fabric dropped to his ankles before he stepped from a leg. He mounted L.J., spreading him despite the bound man's protests and writhing.

L.J. screamed again in fury and desperation.

The man lowered his torso on L.J.'s back, his skin hot and clammy, biting the flesh on the back of his neck and drawing blood.

L.J. cried out as the killer spit out the blood and skin, then leaned further, grabbed L.J. by the hair, yanking his head back as he thrust and bit off L.J.'s lobe. "Who's the alpha, L.J.? Who's the alpha?"

"You are," L.J. bawled. "You are." He buried his face in the grass, repeating submission as his body rocked on the bayou floor.

"You've given me a gift, L.J., one I am prepared to share with the entirety of New Orleans. I am poison. I am vengeance. I've been waiting."

15

When L.J. awoke, the camp dark and deserted. His body and spirit broken, he slowly picked himself up from the ground, limbs screaming in protest, bonds cut. His walk was slow as he staggered and limped.

He stumbled through the swampland and stopped at a small water crossing. He entered the warm waters, trying to wash the blood, filth, and shame from his pores, but none of it seemed to shed. In the darkness, with a glint of the night's light, he watched the floating yellow eyes swim nearer. He had become the hunted. Despite the discomfort, he scrambled from the dangerous waters.

He scampered up the bank, sticking in the mud, and fought against the enveloping swamp. As he lifted a leg, his arm sank. Pushing off with another, his face fell into the muck. He struggled to lift his chin to gasp for breath.

The bellowing growls of alligators near their nests out of sight sent a warning.

L.J. heard the rapid wisps of the grasses and splatters of mud. They were closing in on him.

He splashed frantically, swimming atop the soft ground until he found firm resistance. He pulled himself, his hands fisting the earth to a point where he could raise his legs. He darted forward without a thought, not knowing if he would encounter the ancient monsters as he fled.

He was headed toward the RV when another thought plagued his mind. He'd transferred the curse to a killer who sought the change not for redemption but for evil. It was only after that thought had played out that his own needs entered, and he knew he may never see his family again. Still, he was compelled to seek the root doctor witch for help.

~

THE TREK to the witch's grounds felt endless as he was led not by recall but by intuition. Stamina gone and painfully aware of his nakedness in the wilds, L.J. approached her small, lit cabin, exposed and ashamed. Laying across a porch chair was a thin blanket as though left there just for him. Beside it sat a straw man-sized doll stuffed with Spanish moss adorned with the head of a large alligator.

He wrapped himself in the cloth and gave the light door a rap, which opened the thin wood panel into the modest living quarters.

Draped in a tattered shroud, Aiyana sat among black candles with carved indiscernible words or letters. Her eyes gleamed with other-worldly knowledge. She greeted L.J., her compassion no longer apparent.

"Why have you returned?" She turned a candle upside down, snuffing it out on a plate of dried earth.

L.J. stammered. "I... I think I made a mistake. But no one told me. I didn't know who he was."

Aiyana lowered her eyes. "The spirits will not return your family. You didn't finish the stones." The witch poured a pot of brown putrid water around herself.

"I know." L.J. sat without invitation. "I didn't come for that—I mean, I did, but there's a problem first. I'm afraid he'll go to the city. I need to warn the sheriff. Someone needs to warn the people, like, the whole place. I really think that thing is going to slaughter innocent people. You need to do something. I mean, he's powerful. Like you."

Aiyana nodded. "He's the first. He survived the curse and did what he was required. The spirits have no quarrel when man kills man. Those are laws beyond the swamp, beyond nature. There's nothing to be done. You're free, L.J.; you can go. He isn't bound by the silver ties to his survival. Those fell away with his atonement."

"There has to be something. Someone."

"Nothing. No one."

"But he's created by nature's curse. There has to be something. Can't spirits just shut it off? Say it was a mistake?"

"It was a mistake no more than a snake biting a child or a bear ravaging a town. A beast does what a beast does. They are creatures of nature as the earth intended. He is the wolf; he bows only to the laws of the pack. There is no pack."

L.J. flopped back on the old sofa and closed his eyes. He exhaled, contemplating a whirlwind of thoughts, then resolved himself to words he didn't realize entered his mind. "Me."

Aiyana turned.

"Me. Turn me. Curse me again. Not for my family; he needs to be stopped." L.J. stood. "I'll be the one. He and I aren't through, anyway. I need to do this. I need to try. What else am I going to do? Kill myself? At least I can try to fight."

Eyes glowering. Lips pursed as skeptical. "The spirits knew you would. Let's begin the incantation," she said, standing before L.J., still wrapped. She lifted the small pot of water to his lips. It stank of stagnant rot.

"Wait. Will I be the same? I mean..." His eyes lowered to the ground. "He's—"

"Stronger?" She touched L.J.'s arm, compassion and empathy knowingly returning. "The black one is like a cloak. A blanket. What you wear as a man or beast on the outside is never who you are. We, even as humans, are beasts. Who is Lawrence Thibadeau? What is in your spirit?" She placed a hand over his heart. "You have ancestral spirits of this land, this ground. The Loa are here. Bondye calls your name."

"Stop. This isn't a football game speech; I'm not about to run through a tunnel."

The witch stepped into L.J.'s space and, with a quick tug, yanked away his coverings.

He covered himself immediately. "What the fuck?"

She raked him in a flash with an alligator claw across the chest. "You're afraid he'll mount you again?"

"Shit! Stop. What did you do?" He rubbed at his ripped skin that darkened and hardened like the scales of a reptile.

"You'll feel his dominance in you."

"STOP! Stop saying that." L.J. stepped back toward the door.

"That he'll tear your flesh once more."

"Quit it! Quit saying that."

Aiyana grabbed metal symbols from her walls, symbols of the cursed moon, and hurled them at L.J. "Will he fuck you again like a bitch? Like the weakest of the pack."

"You fucking stop saying that right now." A glint of yellow grew in L.J.'s iris.

The witch chanted in an ancient, guttural tongue, her voice resonating through the bayou, summoning the spirits of the past and rousing them from their everlasting sleep.

"I'm warning you," he growled.

"He fucked you, L.J. You are weak," she spat. "You couldn't stop yourself from killing your own wife, you pathetic weakling of a man."

The ground beneath the shack trembled, and the wails of tormented souls filled the air, kicking up the dust around their feet. It was the ground beneath them that was the last resting place of countless men like him, men who had met their doom by their own hands and whose spirits were bound to the cursed earth.

"I'll kill you!" he spat.

She pursued him with increased aggression. "You ripped the flesh of your own daughter. Ate her entrails. Feasted on her virgin flesh. That innocent child fed your greed! And you lapped it from her purity."

The tortured spirits, like spectral wolves, rose, their mournful howls echoing through the night and shaking the walls. With every mournful howl, they circled closer to L.J., their spectral forms brushing against his trembling body, raising goosebumps with each caress.

Aiyana, eyes ablaze with malevolence, raised her bony hands to the sky. The spirits swirled around L.J., their ethereal forms merging with his flesh, sinking deep into his soul like the roots of an ancient, malicious tree. He screamed in agony as they consumed him, their anguish and fury coursing through his veins.

His eyes glowed with an unholy light, his body twisted and contorted into a monstrous form without the shed and without the pain. He was merged with the wolf in its entirety, no longer Yin and Yang in continual rebirth.

The witch's sinister smile revealed the depths of her wickedness as she had achieved her sinful retribution, and the bayou echoed with the mournful cries of the newly minted beast.

"You mounted their bodies where they—"

With a vicious swipe, the creature lashed at the witch, her head falling under its own weight as the fury of his rage eviscerated her neck.

Her head rolled; eyes still open. From her mouth bubbled blackened swamp water, then came the voice of another. "You are ready. Infect your pack."

16

The night outside of the bayou held the faint scent of jasmine and the glow of the Crescent City's streetlamps. New Orleans was famous for its vibrant nightlife, but that evening was different. A sense of dread hung in the humid air as news quickly spread of a string of gruesome murders occurring on a trail from the rural outskirts toward the city.

Over the past few hours, a serial killer had been terrorizing greater New Orleans. Witnesses reported strange, animal-like howls and victims of all ages being brutally torn apart. The police appeared to be baffled, and the city broadcast its fear of the killing machine lurking in the shadows far and wide.

L.J., like most townspeople and law enforcement, knew the truth. His kind was behind the murders. With each passing moment, the tension grew thicker, choking him until he couldn't stand by any longer.

As he raced through the dim, foggy streets of New Orleans, he could smell the lingering musk of the killer, a sinister blend of blood-lust and fur. His keen senses begged him to take an alternative path and led him to a dilapidated cemetery near the heart of the city.

The atmosphere was electrifying, and as he ventured deeper into the old cemetery where sun bleached stone shone bright. Bone-chilling growls reached his ears. The sound gave him no fear. Instead, it stoked the fire that had sparked within him. To the human ear, it may have sounded like the incoherent grumblings of strung-out street life. To him, it was the unmistakable warning of the pack in the form of homeless Cajuns who had once been under the curse.

L.J. approached the group of sitting and laying men with caution but confidence.

He observed them as they raised their heads, catching his scent in the fair winds. They turned to him, heads and shoulders lowering. Some moved from sitting to lowering to their sides on the ground.

His breath came out in ragged bursts, his eyes wild, and his fur matted by the relentless rain. L.J. growled to assert his prowess in his half-state form, but under kindred spirit.

"I'm no threat," he spoke.

"You ain't 'posed to be out the wilds," one voice said beside him.

L.J. faced the man who clutched a small stuffed animal by his side.

Carrot. The men from the street.

"You?" L.J.'s jaw slackened to disbelief.

Another chuckled. "You so surprised to see us. But ask us if we's surprised. Cuz we ain't. Ain't that right, fellas?"

In unison, they agreed.

"How could you know?" L.J. asked.

"Cuz we all look da same way before we got all caught up."

The men laughed.

The man, Jean, whom L.J. had struck with his vehicle, piped up. "We been talking dat someone bit da wrong boy. We smell him from far apart. He makin' a mess. Ain't no one can do nothing, neither we thought, till you came about. Not sure how dis is even possible to have two'o dem curses running. Dat's a new one to me."

"Dat's new to me, too."

"Me, too," the group chimed.

"We got no time for your kind," one of the Cajun men muttered, squinting through the shadows, his voice rough and thick with the bayou's accent. He was stout, with a thick beard, and his eyes were not just jaundiced but haunted by a history he wanted to forget.

Another man, lean and wiry, spat at L.J.'s feet. "You're cursed, just like we were once, but we've paid our dues. We ain't got nothing to do with that life no more."

The group shared knowing glances and a tense silence hung in the air. The memories of the curse they'd once suffered were still fresh in their minds—the moonlit transformations, the frenzied hunts, the blood on their hands. It was a past they'd worked hard to put behind them and were not eager to be reminded of it.

An older man finally spoke up. "We broke free from that life. We don't intend to go back, not for you or anyone else. You best be on your way, son."

L.J. had expected resistance, but he couldn't walk away, not when the alpha was tearing through the city, leaving a trail of death and destruction in his wake. He had to find a way to convince them.

"I understand. I feel your fear, your desire to leave that dark chapter behind, but you don't know what we're dealing with," L.J. said, his voice pleading, his eyes anguished. "He's a monster, and he won't stop until New Orleans is in ruins."

The Cajun men exchanged uneasy glances, torn between the pain of their past and the present danger looming over their city. The night was thick with tension, and the rain seemed to fall harder as though the heavens were weeping for the city's plight.

The grizzled man, his eyes filled with regret, finally spoke up again. "Tell us more about this alpha. What are we up against?"

L.J. nodded and began recounting the terrifying encounters he'd had with the alpha. He spoke of its size, relentless hunger, and the destruction it left in its wake. He told them about the innocent people who had fallen victim to the beast. With each word, the fire in their eyes began to change from fear to determination.

"But how can we even fight such a creature?" the stout man asked, his voice trembling. "We're just men, not warriors. We don't even have the curse anymore."

They faced a choice—remain in the shadows or confront the darkness once more.

Jean grinned. "If I didn't just has this little spoon and bunny here, I'd go with you."

The others affirmed the same.

The men were strung out. Some were still drug-weary, possibly drunk. Judging by the smell, probably drunk.

"I can turn you back. I don't know for how long. Don't know what'll happen or where you can go after, but I think our job to protect doesn't end where the concrete starts. I—"

"I don't need no speech. Bite my ass. Bite my elbow," one of the crew said.

"Bite us all," declared Jean. "We never paid our full price for what we done did, so time to write more checks. But how you gunna get us with those half-horse teeth?"

Like a flex of a muscle, and without a word, he transformed fully into his beast state. The change caused his bones to crack and his muscles to bulge, but the pain was no longer present.

The men, still hesitant, moved closer to L.J., and one by one, they bared their forearms, offering themselves to the werewolf's bite, accepting the curse once more. As the moon emerged from behind the clouds, their transformation began, their howls echoing through the night, signaling their return as a pack.

Another howl echoed from the city, soon to be the howl of the hunted.

17

L.J. prowled the more darkened and desolate streets of New Orleans honing his senses among the unfamiliar sounds and smells. His ears twitched as he heard the distant cries of the alpha's latest victim. The scent of blood and fear hung heavily in the air, dragging him closer to the scene of the crime. Police sirens and lights were an assault on his heightened sensitivity, and when he closed his eyes momentarily, it enveloped him completely. He retrained focus and pushed on through the noise.

At each street, he found discarded corpses tossed on balconies and left in alleyways, parts strewn about.

He turned down St. Ann Street, following the mayhem.

Another victim, a young woman, lay lifeless in a pool of her own blood, her hair sprawled out around her like a halo. L.J.'s heart sank as he inspected the scene. The alpha had left his gruesome signature of entrail evisceration on this poor soul. Its brutal nature made L.J.'s blood rage with determination. He knew he had to act and put an end to the reign of terror.

As he continued to investigate, a chill ran down his spine. He sensed a presence nearby. It was the alpha, lurking in the shadows.

The beast differed from any he had encountered before. Its eyes burned with a malevolent, crimson glow, and its size was unparalleled. L.J. could sense the overwhelming power radiating from the alpha, and it sent a shiver down his hackles.

The alpha's cruel laughter echoed through the night, chilling L.J. It was as if it could sense the challenge in the air. The time for confrontation had come, and L.J. had to face the blood-soaked beast head-on.

Without hesitation, L.J. let out a long, assertive howl that echoed through the streets of New Orleans. The sound was a call to arms, a declaration of his intent, a direct challenge to the alpha. He was ready to take the fight to the enemy.

The alpha responded, in kind, with an equally threatening wild growl, its footsteps, nails on the asphalt, echoing as it moved closer. Their confrontation was inevitable, and it would take place in the dark, winding streets of the city that had become a battleground.

The two werewolves converged where empty streets opened to what was usually the revelry and vibrant nightlife of Bourbon Street. But this night was desolate and bathed in the pale light of the moon. The alpha emerged from the shadows, blood soaking its fur, eyes fixed on L.J.

L.J. and the alpha circled each other, their growls and snarls filling the street. L.J. was agile and quick, but the alpha's sheer power made it a formidable opponent. It lunged at L.J. with incredible speed, but he narrowly dodged the attack, feeling the alpha's hot breath on his neck.

The alpha spoke, its voice gruff through unused vocal cords. "Come back for more, L.J.? Still trying to win back your dead family from the spirits?"

Ignoring his words, L.J. swiped his knife-like claws at his foe's jawline. A miss.

But as L.J. fought to stop the serial killer, more casualties occurred. Screams filled the night as innocent bystanders stumbled upon the gruesome scene, unable to comprehend the nightmare unfolding before them, and soon found themselves ensnared in the conflict. The killer, caught in a frenzied bloodlust, attacked anything that moved, indiscriminate in its destruction.

L.J. realized that the longer the battle raged, the more lives were at stake. His mission to stop the killer was becoming increasingly perilous, as the beast seemed immune to reason or compassion. They crashed into a nearby storefront, sending shattered glass and debris raining down around them.

Amid the chaos, L.J. had a horrifying realization. The alpha wasn't just a monster; it was a tortured soul trapped in the agonizing torment of their ever-present, ever-shifting transformation, unable to control their predatory instincts. It was driven by an insatiable bloodlust, unable to distinguish friend from foe.

The fight raged on; the two werewolves locked in a deadly dance.

Claws and teeth clashed, fur flew, and blood was spilled. L.J. fought with all his might, but he could feel himself being pushed to the brink. Reinforcements nowhere to be found.

The two werewolves locked eyes in a moment of understanding. In them, L.J. saw the pain and anguish in its gaze, an implicit plea for release from its torment. He realized they may not be so different after all, bound by the same curse.

L.J. made a desperate decision. He would not kill it; he would save it. He lunged at the killer, pinning it to the ground, his massive jaws inches from its throat. The alpha's eyes widened, momentarily in shock, as L.J. hesitated, showing mercy when none was expected. The alpha was just too powerful, too relentless. Its stare hardened and L.J. realized he couldn't show mercy; it was a fight to the death.

The alpha's claws were free and tore into L.J.'s side, drawing blood and fury. L.J. retaliated, snapping his jaws at the killer's throat, only to be met with a brutal counterattack.

L.J. made a desperate move, feigning weakness to lure the alpha in. The maneuver worked, and the alpha pounced, jaws wide open, ready to deliver the final, deadly blow, but L.J. had one last trick up his sleeve.

With a swift and calculated movement, L.J. lunged forward and sank his teeth into the alpha's throat, clamping down with all his strength, tearing everything he could.

The alpha howled in pain and surprise; its crimson eyes full of terror as its life force was threatened. It swiped across L.J.'s belly, who released his hold. The alpha countered with a clawing attack to his eyes.

With a sudden burst of speed, L.J. lunged at the alpha, his jaws clamping onto the larger wolf's throat once more. The alpha struggled and thrashed, but L.J. held on, his grip unyielding. With one final, desperate effort, he sank his teeth deep into the alpha's neck, severing the beast's jugular.

Blood sprayed in a gruesome arc, painting the concrete with a macabre masterpiece. The alpha's eyes widened in horror as it realized its imminent demise until the curse's black magic folded across the wound as their endless cycle of healing and wounding perpetuated.

Not to be bested, the alpha leaped toward the gathered crowd of onlookers. It ripped all within its path, making its way through the panicked fleeing spectators, leaving a trail of blood and body parts in its wake.

As the alpha continued its attack, it heard a different kind of rustling in the shadows. It caught a scent. It could sense movement. It wasn't just one presence; it was multiple. Slowly, figures emerged from the darkness. The pack had held back until a victor was evident.

Their bright yellow eyes were now electrified with rage. They were free and confident of the champion. They were hungry and though they had not forgotten the atrocities they had committed; their humanity was tainted forever. As beasts, they were prime to feed.

The former werewolves encircled the defeated alpha, their eyes filled with determination. They closed in on the beaten blood-soaked beast, once a terrorizing force, it shrank, now the one in peril.

One by one, they attacked, each tearing the wounded killer.

The red glow of its eyes receded, replaced by a haunting, human sadness. Tears welled up as he fought to regain control, the human part of him emerging from the depths of the beast, skin replacing hide, hands replacing claws.

The alpha's mutilated body slumped to the ground, lifeless, motionless. L.J. stood there, panting heavily, his fur matted with blood. The battle had taken its toll, and he had emerged a wounded, exhausted warrior. But he had achieved his goal. The blood-soaked alpha was defeated, and New Orleans could finally breathe a sigh of relief.

The pack headed off to the bayou, with L.J. staying behind. He needed to take care of something at home.

As the first rays of dawn broke, the killer reverted fully to his human form. Redemption, in the end, was nothing more than killers receiving a chance to kill and live with their curse rather than succumb to it in isolated grief.

18

L.J. returned to the place he had called home for all of one night. The house stood silent, a solemn reminder of the tragedy that had befallen his family. Police tape no longer surrounded the perimeter. There were no flashing sirens, milling investigators or a congested crowd of onlookers hoping for a glimpse of horror.

L.J. stepped carefully, staying close to the tall landscaping as he made his discrete approach, heart heavy as he looked at the almost-familiar façade of the house. The white picket fence held a very different dream from the nightmare that had unfolded within. The windows remained shattered, a testament to the night when every-thing changed.

There remained "Do Not Enter" tape at the back door. The lock had not been replaced, and the door opened with little more than a slight push. Unpacked boxes still sat in the various rooms, neglected and forgotten. Some of them, however, bore the evidence of that night, with dried blood spatters soaked into the cardboard. They were a chilling reminder of the violence that had taken place within those walls.

Beignet powder dusted the table and chair. If he squinted, he could still make out tiny sticky fingerprints.

The house that was meant to be their forever home had never lived up to that promise. It was just an empty shell, forever devoid of his family's life or happiness. L.J. could never live there anymore, not after what he had seen, endured, and committed.

With a heavy sigh, he entered the living room, his footsteps echoing down the empty halls. The air felt stagnant and heavy. The room had become a muggy and desolate space. The walls, never adorned with their family photos, remained bare.

L.J. made his way upstairs, guided by the distant echoes of his wife's and daughter's voices. The bedroom they had shared for one night was the most painful to enter. The bed was neatly made. L.J. reached out and ran his fingers over the crumpled sheets as if hoping to find some trace of his loved ones, even wishing that Taylor Swift's songs would play again.

Unable to bear the pain of the cold bed any longer, he moved to the boxes that contained their belongings. He had a purpose: locating a small silver object that held a deep significance. Lon had told him he needed to find it, that it was the key to unlocking the next step after shattering his life.

L.J. sifted through the boxes, memories flooding back with every item he touched. He found his wife's jewelry, more of his daughter's stuffed animals, and his own keepsakes. Each item was a snapshot of a happier time before darkness had descended.

As he continued to search, he came across a small silver locket. It was delicate and intricately engraved, with a tiny keyhole on the back. One he had given to Gwen for Valentine's Day a year after marriage. L.J. held it in his trembling hands, his heart pounding with anticipation.

Just as he was about to pocket it, a voice startled him. "L.J.," the sheriff said, his tone filled with empathy. He had quietly entered the house, understanding the pain and turmoil that L.J. was going through.

L.J. faced the sheriff, his eyes red and tired from sleepless nights and tears. "Sheriff," he acknowledged, his voice hollow.

"We got a call that there was a break-in. Figured it was you. They always come back. Figured you would, too, especially after the night you had. Not sure how it all transpired, but it seems like you really came through." The sheriff stepped further into the room, his gaze filled with understanding. "I know it's difficult being back here, L.J.," he said with genuine affection. "But I have to ask, what are you planning to do now?"

L.J. didn't hesitate. "I need to get a couple things," he replied, his grip on the locket tightening. "This locket should do. I think it's my time to say goodbye."

The sheriff nodded in agreement. "I understand. Frankly, I'd try to talk you out of it, but after what happened here and the events in the Quarter, you're connected. You'll be held accountable and always seen as dark and dangerous. The world won't know how to deal with that if you're found and know you can change. Videos of that whole thing are already flooding the interweb and social media. Fortunately, most will think it's faked by all that computer stuff. You've already put yourself in harm's way by helping us stop that murderer. I get your wanting to step aside."

L.J. met the sheriff's gaze, his determination unwavering. "It's for the best."

The sheriff respected L.J.'s resolve, eyes softer than ever. "I understand, and I won't stand in your way, but you should know that if you change your mind, this road may lead to even more danger. If you need help, don't hesitate to reach out. We'll be there for you and do our best to put you somewhere remote as long as you hold up your bargain and never come back to the city."

L.J. nodded in gratitude, appreciating the sheriff's support. "Thank you, Sheriff. I'll keep that in mind."

The two men stood in the quiet room, united by a shared understanding of the nightmares that lurked in the shadows.

"What do I do with all this?" L.J. asked.

The sheriff put his hands on his hips and looked around. "We, or let's say the state, have a way of handling such things. It'll be sold. Contents are given to the homeless or less fortunate. I think 'less privileged' is the phrase we're meant to use. Monies will be put into a New Orleans reparation fund. There are many oddities in this area that get swept under the rug. Those funds tend to help things just go away."

As L.J. continued to hold the small silver locket in his hand, he felt a tingling inside. A small surge of determination and new resolve. The memories of his family were worth the fight, and he was willing to continue his own sacrifice to bring justice to those he had lost. He dropped the silver back in the box. He'd overplayed the selfish coward's hand.

"Maybe you could drive me back to the RV, and we could talk about how I can help you out. Maybe help with these oddities."

The sheriff pat L.J. on the back. "You're a local, L.J.. We're happy to have you."

19

Days later, L.J. returned to his duty as watcher and protector.

The night, like so many under L.J.'s watch, was the start of renewed threats to the waters and wetlands.

With no visible moon, the late evening grew increasingly darker, as if the heavens were conspiring to unleash a torrent of terror upon the Earth. The winds howled like the lamentations of the damned, and the distant rumble of thunder resonated like the growls of yet another vengeful beast. A supernatural storm brewed over the ancient burial mound that had long been a source of mystery in the small, remote bayou area he continued to traverse.

The townsfolk had always known to avoid the burial mound, the sinister, moss-covered hillock well beyond the edge of the swamp. It was said to be the last resting place of those who had been condemned by some long-forgotten curse, their souls forever trapped beneath the earth. The stories told around campfires spoke of restless spirits and unexplainable phenomena that plagued anyone who dared to tread near the mound after nightfall, notwithstanding the Rougarou.

L.J. had finally learned to live in harmony with the natural world, walking the line between human and wolf as guardian of the forest. But his life remained marred by tragedy committed by his own hand. Heartbroken and no longer seeking vengeance, he took on the wolf form permanently, leaving his human life behind.

As the storm gathered strength, L.J. felt an irresistible pull, a call from the depths of the mound. The winds whispered secrets to him like they had in the past, and the earth trembled beneath his paws. He knew he had to answer the call, for it felt like a force greater than himself was drawing him back to the mound.

Ignoring the rain and lightning that streaked across the sky, L.J. approached the burial mound with fright and anticipation. It radiated an energy unlike any he'd experienced before, its surface covered in ancient symbols that glowed. He hesitated momentarily, knowing that the place had birthed nothing but doom and despair.

Despite his apprehension, the call was too strong, and L.J. could not resist. With a final deep breath, he approached the mound and pressed his massive wolf body against its side. The earth quaked beneath him, reverberating through his bones, and the mound began to shift and crumble as if nature were tearing it asunder.

The supernatural storm raged on, reaching its crescendo as the mound cracked open, revealing a dark, gaping chasm beneath. He approached the mound and knelt before it, fur sodden like the earth under him.

L.J. watched in awe and apprehension as the earth gave birth to a mother wolf and her young kit. They emerged from the depths of the mound, their fur glistening with an unearthly radiance.

The mother wolf was a majestic creature, her eyes filled with peace and wisdom. The young kit, barely more than a pup, was a bundle of energy and curiosity, bounding around the mound and staring only briefly back to the abyss they'd just emerged from before turning to L.J. They both possessed an aura of power and mystery that left L.J. in a state of wonder.

As the storm raged on, the mother wolf and her kit began to howl, mournful cries blending with the fury of the wind and rain. It was a haunting sound, and he could feel the ancient spirits of the mound awakening, their presence heavy in the air.

L.J. watched as the mother wolf and her kit circled the mound, their movements graceful and purposeful. It was as if they were paying homage to the spirits that had granted them life, and L.J. realized that they were no ordinary wolves. They were creatures of the supernatural, brought forth from the burial mound by forces beyond his understanding.

Then, to his amazement, the mother wolf turned her gaze toward him. Her eyes locked onto his, and a sense of deep recognition passed between them. She knew him; it was as if they shared a bond that transcended the boundaries of time and space.

At that moment, L.J. felt a surge of hopeful emotion. It was a mixture of joy and a profound sense of longing. He knew in his heart that they were his lost loved ones, reborn from the earth by the spirits of the burial mound.

Tears welled in L.J.'s amber eyes as he realized the supernatural storm had granted him a second chance. He lowered to the ground, his wolf form able to convey his heart overflowing with love and gratitude.

The mother wolf and her kit approached him, eyes filled with understanding and acceptance. They nuzzled against him, and L.J. pawed at them as his fur returned once more.

As the storm continued to rage around them, L.J. knew that he had been given a precious gift, a chance to rebuild the life he'd lost. He would protect them with every ounce of his being, and honor the spirits of the burial mound that had brought them back to him for the rest of his life.

But he also understood that their existence was a delicate balance between the realms of the living and the supernatural. For that moment, though, they were together, and nothing else mattered. As the storm subsided, the supernatural energies that had brought them together slowly faded. The burial mound closed once more, concealing its secrets beneath the earth.

L.J. remained with his family, the rain washing away the tears on his lupine face. He knew their journey was just beginning, and he was ready to face whatever challenges lay ahead.

A volley of shots rang out from the foliage under the departing mystical storm.

The wolves yipped then fell into a heap, the larger wolves writhing in pain.

The pup lay on its side lifeless, save for the slow rise of her rib cage, as the mother wolf tried to paw closer.

The mother dragged her hind legs, back broken. Intent on reaching the little one, she nevertheless succumbed quickly to her mortal wounds with a brief shutter, not making it more than a few deep claw marks in the earth.

From the tree line broke two men, high-fiving one another and racing to the carcasses. L.J. lay panting from his wounds, eyes fixed on his renewed family whose eyes slowly rolled back into their skulls.

The hunters neared; their exuberance palpable. They soon hovered over him, gawking and excited.

"This one's still alive? Should we cap him?"

"Hang on. Let me get my hat and glasses. Get your camera ready."

The hunter placed a camo ball cap between L.J.'s long, pointed ears. Followed by sunglasses that rested atop his long nose. The hunter leaned in for the photo. "Wait, get in. Selfie."

"Here, get in closer to him. Wrap that front leg around you like we're all pals."

"Hang on, I'm gunna hold up his jowls so he gives us a big toothy smile."

"Granny, what big teeth you have," a hunter laughed. "Wait, toss me that little pup. Family photo with his little me."

The hunters lay the pup against L.J., its small heart beat now still. L.J. loosed a mournful whimper.

"Hurry up, the wolf's saying take the fucking picture. He can't hold that smile forever."

"Say, hashtag LJTalbotHunts. I'm going to tag him and see if he responds."

The two hunters leaned in for the shot.

Flash.

"Fuck!" The hunter screamed, snatching his bleeding hand inward.

L.J.'s eyes narrowed as he rose.

~

End

ABOUT THE AUTHOR

J.T. Patten is an emerging author of horror stories. This is J.T.'s eighth dark fiction book. He is an active member of the Horror Writers Association and International Thriller Writers. His initial best-selling works have gained acclaim for their "blacker than black" brooding narrative that illuminate the blurred lines in life and twist traditional tropes on their head.

He has a degree in Foreign Language, a Masters in Strategic Intelligence, graduate studies in Counter Terrorism from the University of St. Andrews.

More information about JT and his works can be found at www.jtpattenbooks.com

ALSO BY J.T. PATTEN

Horror

Brothers of Blood

The Hidden (WIP)

Thrillers

Shadow Masters

Primed Charge

Presidential Retreat

Buried in Black

Presence of Evil

Made in the USA
Monee, IL
17 November 2024

70404897R00079